Praise for FERAL

"A joyously quiet and unruly novel that yearns and grieves for our lost origins and defies us — with a humor so gentle that it hurts — to explore the uncertain shapeshifting boundaries between what we think is animal and what we assume is humanity, demanding that we climb the tree of existence and stay there until we understand what comes next, what must come next, what might possibly save us from extinction."

— Ariel Dorfman, author of *Death and the Maiden*

"There aren't many people who could do what Deena Metzger did — and then find the language to tell us about it. She tracks the healing process with unusual precision and insight. This is an extraordinary story of becoming whole from a wise healer and a humble seeker."

— Ellen Bass, author of *The Human Line*

"This book is good medicine."

— Larry Dossey, MD, author of *Healing Words* & *The Power of Premonitions*

"With tremendous insight and compassion, Deena Metzger's unique book leads us into the intuitive depths of a profound therapeutic relationship. In her breathtaking and poetic prose, Feral leads us on a truly remarkable and beautiful engagement with the wild journey that is healing."

— Lewis Mehl-Madrona, MD, author of *Coyote Medicine*

"Deena Metzger's *Feral* is a fascinating account of the unfolding relationship between a traumatized, courageous young woman and a wisely humble counselor/healer. Almost an allegory, this tale illuminates the ever changing ground of interdependence and vulnerability between what is traditionally seen as the helper and the one who is helped, as well as between the human and other species. Essentially, the mostly invisible pathways that connect all beings are revealed. As a psychologist, as a poet, and as a seeker of spiritual understanding, I was completely entranced."

— Shirley Graham, author of *What Someone Wanted*

"Part myth, part tale, half dream, half rooted in life as we know it — *the devastating real* — Metzger's *Feral* forces us to confront our ideas of love and offers a challenging map of what it means to truly transform. Her spare but provocative character, Azul, will never leave you, and neither will the path she lays at your feet; the one that says *come this way if you dare*, for she knows as few do that it leads directly to the place of danger where the heart must take a leap."

— Peter Levitt, recipient of the Lannan Foundation Award in Poetry; author of *Within Within* and other books of poetry and prose

"How do we perceive and change our personal and cultural constructs? In *Feral*, poet, therapist, social activist, Deena Metzger, herself a master shapeshifter, upon meeting Azul, a girl/sprite/animal spirit, attempts to empty herself of her assumptions and presumptions so she might have a relationship with the 'other.' Azul, the 'other,' asks her only to be 'real.' To be authentic in relationship with ourselves and with the other is a great challenge and the great learning. *Feral* describes Deena's subtle explorations of her human arrogance, as she shifts from her egocentric thinking patterns to a kinesthetic awareness ('she began to read the aromas as carefully as she had read print') which allows her to enter the possibility of connection to a larger world. The story is both an exquisitely written parable and a riveting adventure into the awakening of the soul."

— Diane Wolkstein, author of *Inanna, Queen of Heaven and Earth*

"On a tightrope stretched between enlightenment and oneness with nature on the one hand and injury and madness on the other, *Feral* teeters wildly. Its central theme: what is healing and who needs it most — the hunter or the hunted, the animal or humankind, the therapist or the patient? Our brains are said to contain three layers — a reptilian base, layered by a mammalian ring, covered by a uniquely human neocortex. If you think the human cortex is really on top, *Feral* will set you straight. In a spark and glimmer of flash and transformation Metzger dips us into the primordial soup, spins us around counter-clockwise, back to the beginning of time. We are then stripped of clothes and ordinary comforts in order to seek the wisdom and self-knowledge locked into the pain that can't and shouldn't be taken away. Instead we must shimmy up the world tree fully naked in order to reconnect with our animal eyes, piss and howl."

— Terry Marks-Tarlow, author of *Psyche's Veil: Psychotherapy, Fractals and Complexity*

"Thousands upon thousands of writers have obeyed the old dictum to "put your characters up a tree, shake things at them, and then bring them down again," but leave it to Deena Metzger to achieve this task in such a profoundly literal and exuberantly figurative way. Articulating a near-unfathomable experience with an uncommonly nuanced depth of feeling and thought, Feral has the wild, dark humor and sustained intensity of a brilliantly compressed fever-dream. It's the diamond in this author's diadem of fiction."

— Billy Mernit, author of *Imagine Me and You*

FERAL

OTHER WORKS BY DEENA METZGER

Ruin and Beauty: New and Selected Poems
Doors: A Fiction for Jazz Horn
The Other Hand
What Dinah Thought
The Woman Who Slept With Men to Take the War Out of Them
A Sabbath Among the Ruins
Looking for the Faces of God

NON-FICTION

From Grief Into Vision: A Council
Entering the Ghost River: Meditations on
the Theory and Practice of Healing
Writing For Your Life: A Guide and Companion to the Inner Worlds
Tree: Essays and Pieces

FERAL

A novel by

Deena Metzger

HAND TO HAND

Hand to Hand is a community based endeavor that supports independently published works and public events, free of the restrictions that arise from commercial and political concerns. It is a forum for artists who are in dynamic and reciprocal relationship with their communities for the sake of peacemaking, restoring culture and the planet. For further information regarding Hand to Hand please write to us at: P.O. Box 186, Topanga, CA, 90290, USA. Or visit us on the web at:

www.handtohandpublishing.com

Donations to organizations have been made to replenish the trees that were used to create the paper in this book. We also wish to acknowledge the RSF Social Finance AnJel Donor Advised Fund for their support.

FERAL. Copyright © 2011 by Deena Metzger

Manufactured in the USA by Hand to Hand.
Hand to Hand First Edition, February, 2011
05 04 03 02 01
ISBN: 978-0-9720718-5-7

Book and Cover Design: Stephan David Hewitt
Cover Inset Painting by Pami Ozaki

Hand to Hand Publishing
P.O. Box 186
Topanga, CA 90290

Publisher's Cataloging-in-Publication Data

Metzger, Deena.
　　Feral / Deena Metzger.
　　p. cm.
　　ISBN-13: 978-0-9720718-5-7
　　ISBN-10: 0-9720718-5-7

　　1. Feral children--Fiction. 2. Social norms--Fiction. 3. Self-consciousness (Awareness)--Fiction. 4. Psychological fiction. I. Title.

PS3563.E864F47 2011　　　　813'.54
　　　　QBI11-600025

For Pami Blue Hawk Ozaki,
Her Beauty and Her Inspiration

The moment it first occurred to the woman that she would bring the girl home was when the girl had climbed to a sturdy branch halfway up the sycamore and ensconced herself there, first removing, then dropping, her yellow leather work boots and then her socks, stretched out like lilies at their tops, fluorescent lime green no less. The girl wrapped what looked like prehensile toes around some of the finer twigs so that it appeared that she had grown into the tree or it into her. When the woman was trying to discern the nature of the being she was examining, first she thought feral, then thinking feral, she thought wolf. But wolves don't climb trees, both the girl and the woman knew that.

Confronted by the girl's feet, she was compelled to say simian, ape, primate, mono, monkey, but stopped there as no one would identify a species by its feet alone. Then as the woman teetered between one identification and another without knowing if the confusion or complexity was in the girl or in herself, the girl raised her mouth to the sky and opened it into a fluted goblet as if to catch rain. The sadness the child exuded was so like a perfume that one could not bear taking it in or being without it. Grief eased out into the air extending itself in mineral colors like oil on water, the thinnest of diaphanous films until it found its destination and wrapped itself about the living body, a sculpture in opal and mother of pearl. So many days, the woman admitted, she had been curious about grief while most willing to avoid the textures of its mysteries.

Climbing the tree had not been a thoughtless or impetuous action. The girl had taken a Jew's harp, a handful of dried cranberries, a scrap of blue leather, feathers, a vial of silver and turquoise beads, a needle, some thread, other secret objects, some sacred, all carefully balanced in the lap of an oversized T-shirt that the girl turned alternately into a desk, a knapsack, a handkerchief for blowing her nose, while another T-shirt became a bandanna, a snood, and a white banner that declared most adamantly: "I will not surrender."

Closer scrutiny indicated however that this was not a wolf or a monkey person. Nothing so close to human. Or so diminished as to say humanoid. No protoperson. Nor was she any animal the woman could identify, but she was of another species, the woman thought, of another species altogether. The way the words fell together, something else she could not yet understand was presented to her mind: An animal of other species altogether. Or, as she was only later to understand the meaning of: an animal of other species all together.

The stone fell with enough force that there was no doubt it had been aimed and thrown to land exactly three inches from the woman's foot.

The girl was known to bite. Or so, Carmela who had taken the girl in, alleged. The woman eased herself down against the trunk of the tree. So the girl had thrown a stone. It hadn't hit the woman. The miss was deliberate. It was an ardent signal although its meaning was unclear. Fundamentally, it indicated — "watch out." OK. She would sit down and watch. Out. Out of herself. Watch to see what would happen next.

The least sensible thing to do would be to get a ladder and climb up the tree. The girl was fast and nimble, as any tree-based animal might be. Even if she succeeded in reaching the girl before the girl pushed her down or climbed higher or fell down herself, what would be accomplished? She could hardly expect to have a sensible conversation with the girl up there in the branches. They had never really succeeded at conversations when Carmela had brought the girl to see the woman and the woman had always known that she was not agile enough to corner the girl in the house, had it ever been necessary.

Nor was it a good idea to call the fire department. The girl would scratch, tear, kick, twist, slap, chew, spit. The woman could not pretend the girl was a house cat, or an escaped parakeet. Every morning a flock of green parrots swept through the neighborhood, a gang of runaways accommodating to the foliage and the weather. This girl was a loner. No virtue in treating her as if she were a member of a flock, or a herd animal, or a rabid dog, or worse, a wild animal, a big cat, escaped from its confines, from the zoo, and needing to be behind bars, "for its own sake," as people were likely to say.

"Would you like to come down?" the woman asked trying to be sensible and to establish herself as someone who knew how to behave under such circumstances.

"It is beautiful up here," the girl said. "If you climb up we can have a picnic. I have…" and then she looked through her treasures, holding each object up to the light, "nothing much to eat really. You'll have to bring your own. Bring hot dogs."

Wolf, the woman thought again.

"And fruit."

Raccoon, the woman postulated.

"Tortillas."

Coyote.

"*No soy coyote.*" Had the girl whispered this or was the woman imagining this? If she wasn't a coyote, the woman might be safe with her.

The girl was rummaging through her treasures again and yes, there was the knife in the sheath attached to a belt. She put it on as if it was the most natural adornment.

The woman hesitated and then continued as if nothing had changed between them.

"Would you like me to come up? I guess I can manage it." She didn't mean it. She couldn't imagine how she would get up there, but she thought it was worth asking.

"You can't come up," the girl said. "This is my country." It was a definitive statement. "Don't try it." She paused. "I know you won't anyway. You don't know how to come here."

The girl knew more about the woman than the woman knew about the girl. What would she bring the girl if they were going to have a picnic? Food with a lot of vitamin B in it, the woman thought. Food for the nervous system. She was thinking of greens and brown rice when other thoughts, decidedly foreign on practical and culinary grounds, made a dramatic entry: hearts of palm, maguey blossoms marinated in lime and tossed with red and yellow nasturtiums in a nest of rice on a bed of leaves, miner's lettuce with the sweet coral berries of the Australian pepper tree, cactus with red hot chilies, angel's hair with lemon butter, pansies and rose petals. Such an invasion of mind had to be accounted for. The girl was infiltrating the woman's mind.

"Do you like to eat flowers?"

The girl looked startled and blushed several shades of bougainvillea — magenta, crimson, purple, orange, then pale white. For an instant, the woman had her.

"Oleander is poisonous. Watch out." The words appeared in the woman's mind as on a computer screen, so she didn't know if they were hers or the girl's.

Then two elderly women, Carmela and her housemate, Dusty, appeared. Until the girl climbed the tree, Carmela, who had invited the girl to live with her, had willingly shared the house and yard where the girl had been camping out between the worlds. Now they were walking in a file, Carmela extending a plate of cookies and Dusty, with equal solemn formality, offering a glass of fresh squeezed orange juice. Carmela held up a cookie, timorously, reaching toward the girl and backing away, simultaneously.

"I don't think she'll bite," the woman said. "She's not an animal, you know," she said, wondering what she meant to convey with this adamant statement when, of course, she was certain the girl would bite.

"Don't be so certain." Carmela, who knew the girl's ways had called the woman, though she had waited longer than Dusty would have liked. Now they both wanted the girl down from the tree. They wanted the woman to take her away. They wanted. "Hold on to her," they said. "Don't let her get away. Don't ..."

"I'll put her on a leash," the woman said exasperated even though the two women had been quite kind, or so the girl had said when they had brought the unwilling girl to the woman's house. "To talk" was the euphemism they had used each time they left the girl for an hour or so. Then it had seemed to the woman that the girl was as reluctant and confused as an animal brought for its own good to be probed or vaccinated by a vet.

A memory emerged so swiftly the woman felt a bit of vertigo and lost her inner balance as she teetered between the present and the past, then and now. When she'd been a girl of seven, a three-year-old boy who lived across the street had been kept on a leash by his mother. One end of a cord some fifteen feet long had been tied to the porch railing while the other end was hitched around his waist and shoulders to allow the boy the range from house to curb. The little boy wandered up and down the stairs and back and forth on the sidewalk, sometimes winding himself around the sycamore in the front yard, after which, for long stretches of time, he cried piteously for his mother to free him from immobility. It was true that she was only seven at the time but she had never forgiven herself for watching this scene play out again and again and doing nothing about it. Something about the boy's predicament had seemed to her so very frightening that she had been afraid to approach him even when he only needed to be unwound or when he had climbed, leash and all, into a wood playpen, snuggling up against the bars, so distraught was he. Had she thought he would bite? It wasn't that alone. The child was so bereft, his situation so degraded, his mother so much angrier than the other mothers who only said they were at the end of their rope, that if she, as a little girl, could have put words to her fear, she would have said that the circuit of rope which circumscribed the boy's movements was one of the rivers surrounding hell and anyone who entered it ran the risk of drowning or remaining on that desolate shoreline forever.

The woman was older now and not so afraid of catching the girl's grief.

"Who is she?" the woman asked. "Did you ever find out anything about her? Where does she come from? Who are her people?"

"She belongs to no one," Carmela answered, either dismissing the girl, or condemning her.

"Then she belongs to herself?"

"That's no one." Dusty whispered in her little rag of a voice.

"Actually," Dusty continued, self-righteously, "I know something about her. Or rumors." She lowered her voice and came up to the woman so that the girl wouldn't overhear what was being said unless, as the woman suspected, she had the sharp hearing of an animal. "They say her father was a ... They say, her mother .... They say she ran away from home and was never found. They say she lived on her own in the mountains."

Not to be outdone, Carmela shouldered Dusty aside to commandeer the woman's attention, "Some say, a jaguar raised her."

The two women turned away and then turned back, each with the same stunned expression that revealed for the first time that they really didn't know why they had taken the girl in. They didn't know anything really except now the girl was in the tree, had been there for hours and they were up a tree about knowing what to do.

Carmela, panicked, had called the woman who had been talking to the girl occasionally for several weeks at Carmela's request. The woman hadn't asked, "How can I help?" She had just come.

Now Carmela and Dusty were looking at the woman with kindness. And hope. They wanted the girl out.

The woman asked for food and sat quietly, as if there were no girl in a tree, no wolf, no apparitions. Dutifully, the two women brought coffee and another glass of orange juice and also hot dogs and a platter of sliced fruit, mango, papaya, melon. On another plate were circles of *queso blanco* on tiny tortilla rounds arranged around fresh salsa which, the woman surmised, the girl had made herself before she climbed the tree.

The women went back into their house, having agreed to leave for several hours, to see a movie. Then there was a sound of a car starting up and driving away.

"Did you hear them leave?" the woman asked the girl. "They have left the two of us to each other."

There was no answer from the tree. Silence.

"There's juice and cookies here whenever you want them." She looked for a way to pass them up so that the girl could get them without endangering herself, without having to risk being caught by the woman, but there was no branch close enough upon which she could balance a plate. "Hot dogs too. Tortillas. Fruit. Juice. Cookies. You conjured all of it." Pause. "Any time you're hungry." Silence. "You must be hungry. I can tell. I'm certain of it." Silence. As if the girl had really disappeared.

The woman found herself looking to see if any of the branches led to other trees in the yard, checking out avenues of escape, even for a split second entertaining the mad idea that the girl could fly. But then she found her, or a smudge of her, a smear of brown flesh on a long white mottled limb, an aggregate of rage and terror held together in the shape of foot, thigh, rump. It was all she could see. A hunted animal. A frightened creature. Just as she settled in, all the girl's remaining clothes, except for the white banner came down from that living burl in the tree with a thump.

The woman prepared for a long wait. Being that it was a warm May afternoon, the woman took her light jacket and rolled it into a pillow for the hollow at the small of her back. If it was not for the fact that she understood that the girl was suffering, she would say that the girl had appeared at exactly the right time. The woman was tired of human chatter. She would spend the night at the base of the tree waiting for the girl. She could spend a week if necessary. As it happened, she was on vacation. She might as well spend it here. Eventually the girl would come down if only to see if the unoccupied portion of the nest of leaves at the foot was more comfortable than the sky nest she had made for herself at the crook where the largest branch veered out toward the horizon.

The girl would descend in a manner befitting the kind of animal she was. The woman did not think she was dealing with a mammal of sloth nature or bat nature who preferred trees to earth. She had already established in her mind that this was no monkey though the girl had cradled herself against the trunk exactly as an alpha male Capuchin had done when the woman had observed him sleeping in a sitting position while the females and the younger ones stretched out on the branches below. The woman had spent days at Rincon Vieja in Costa Rica watching monkeys in the way she was watching the girl now. After a few days, she had told the lover who was traveling with her, "I want to die here. I want to come here when I am mortally ill in order to watch the monkeys in the trees as I die."

At some time in the past, human ancestors had come down from the trees to explore the savannas. It had occurred at the same time that color had entered the landscape. One could say that all of human history followed from that. What she knew about the girl from hearsay and her own limited contact with her, the few times the girl had come — or rather had been brought — to her house, indicated that trees were not her habit of choice, but rather that they, like a dark corner, cave or closet, provided escape as well as a vantage point.

The woman began to think about the kinds of animals that secured their lives in caves and those that secured their lives in trees. To defend a cave, the creature would have to be powerful, fierce. Tree security did not require strength. It required one to be light, lithe, and agile.

"Do you ever fly in your dreams?"

"I stay awake in my dreams. I always have to be alert. Sometimes I fly ... away."

The girl was alert. She exhibited a creature instinct to protect herself through bravado, wariness and seclusion. Interests in food and water were clearly secondary. Survival had to do with escape or making herself invulnerable. From this the woman drew certain conclusions: During the history of her life, the girl had suffered more from being accessible than from being hungry.

What tactics she had developed over the years to protect herself would soon become clear. She was armed, obviously. She probably had a cache of stones hidden away in little niches in the trunk or in the forks between the branches. The woman had been told that the girl always carried a knife in a leather sheath strapped to her belt but also that she was more likely to use it against herself in a ceremony of bloodletting than against others. Weapons didn't seem to be the main line of defense.

The knife, her seeming defense, was her jeopardy. There was a fragility, or an illusion of fragility, so that, instinctively, one wanted to protect her.

Yes, her jeopardy was her defense. She was so engaging, one would not take arms against her. She was enchanting. Or enchanted. It was as if the girl had gathered all creatures into herself. As if wolf, monkey, bird had become one creature, all together, one phantasmagoria, a magical beast, an original like a sphinx. One could not take one's eyes off her, and yet one couldn't see her clearly either. One's hands locked around smoke.

A shapeshifter. I've got myself a shapeshifter, the woman thought. At first she was pleased as if she had made a conquest and then she was a bit ashamed of thinking she had triumphed. Then she looked at her hands and saw they were empty. There was nothing in the tree but vapors and in contrast she felt massive, as if she wasn't a creature either, but in contrast to the shimmering volatility of the girl, she was simply dull, heavy clay from which something might someday be made, with the girl's help. She settled down, ass on the ground, to wait.

But she couldn't wait in silence. It wasn't her style. She listened for the girl's mind. She listened for squawks and trills, for chattering, for monkey mind. She would know it if the girl was so afflicted, even if it was only the tremors of the twigs she heard rustling according to the girl's quick thoughts. The girl was absolutely silent. Her mind was still.

The only sounds the woman heard were the consequence of her own inner prolixity. A din of associations bumbled through her mind. Adam and Eve. The stage was set. They were in a garden. There was a tree. The tree was hiding the girl. The woman was hungry for something. All that was needed was a serpent. Someone to say, "Dare."

My mind's a blithering mess, the woman thought. Primal ooze. My God, what's happening to me. What game is this child playing with me?

On cue, the girl sidled back and forth on the heavy limb she had chosen as her perch. She wrapped herself around it. She rolled around it. Snake was added to the retinue of creatures that composed her. The woman was trying to wrap her mind around the phenomenon of the girl when a sound issued from the girl's mouth, clatter of beads on a calabash, a warning rattle.

"Don't try to read my mind," the girl said. "I don't want to have to fill it with junk just to confuse you."

Strategy one had failed. On to strategy two. The woman leaned back into the tree contemplating the soft bowl formed by her own belly, thighs and forearms. In her mind, her hand smoothed the clay, flicking drops of pure water onto flattened mud coils, until she was such a vessel that the girl would not be able to resist and so she would climb down from the tree to curl into the artfully crafted nest, head in the woman's lap. And then if the woman was careful enough she would raise her arm, but not so much for the girl to fear a blow, and would place it on the girl's long shining black hair braided with the leaves and blue feathers she had gathered from the sycamore. And stroke her hair. Then if the girl allowed it: singing.

Of course it happened exactly when she was caught in such an idyllic reverie, when she was lost in fantasies of her own irresistible benevolent presence, to nurture without altering, to interact without affecting, to touch without marking, to offer without wanting, to protect without domesticating, to listen without intruding, to extend without penetrating, to enact her unique and exemplary ability to tame the wild without taming the wild, that the girl let loose with a pungent, yellow stream of urine that was not, as was the stone, designed to miss the mark. The thrill of mink was that it might, could, did — often — bite.

Naïvely, the woman had reckoned that the girl would not relieve herself while in the tree, that she would not piss on her head. This turned out not to be correct. The woman did not know anything about the girl. But she saw this: The girl was not out of control. Despite this incident, the girl was always fastidious. She had let go with precise, exact marksmanship.

It was thrilling. What was thrilling? Being pissed on didn't thrill the woman. It had some currency in pornography, she had heard, being pissed on. A male thing usually. The fast path of the eros of degradation. The man would inveigle a woman to piss on him. It wasn't to correct the usual order of history, it was .... She didn't know what it was and her lover had confided that a woman he knew had insisted he piss on her. Then as he had found himself intrigued, he immediately got out of bed, put on his clothes and walked out the door, reeking with self-righteousness.

Once with her lover... in a little clearing in the woods... near a river... it was a warm evening. A stream nearby. On each other's feet. They had let go at once.

"My siblings taught me," the girl inserted herself into the woman's mind. "My older sister taught my two older brothers and I taught the youngest one who was five when I was six. It was easier for the boys. I had to learn to aim. I got so good at it, I was the champ even if I didn't have the best equipment."

"So don't try to get control of the situation," the girl hissed aloud. "I may not have a pot to piss in, but I don't need one," she said with absolute dignity.

The woman knew her hair could be washed. Clothes could be washed. Urine was sterile. She pretended to herself that she found this comforting. In fact, she did find the urine comforting. That is, it set parameters broader than she had expected. It expanded the playing field. She burrowed down into the soft earth under her and adjusted her jacket. Yes, she would wait the girl out. And she had a strategy too.

She would wait for the women to return from the movies. She would put the girl in their hands for the night. They could sleep on the porch. They wouldn't need to stay awake to keep watch as it was, given the last scene, most unlikely that the girl would come down while they were outside since the girl had climbed the tree to escape them in the first place. Success. The woman had the girl treed.

The woman settled back again against the tree but more carefully this time. Careful, that is, about what was in her mind. And this led her to wonder what in fact was in her mind. Was there anything in her mind that belonged to her? Or was everything in her mind something she had gathered or been given by others? Was there anything in her mind about the girl and what they were doing there together that was her own thought? Was her mind her own or did it belong to others?

It was a May afternoon. She was sitting under a tree. The girl had clearly decided there was nothing better to do. At this point, she almost faltered again by thinking of how the girl had brought her to this extremity. For it was extremity. Sitting in the damp of someone else's piss was not extremity; she'd suffered many inconveniences and discomforts for others' sakes over the years. But sitting at the base of a tree with no intention of doing anything else, this was for her an extremity.

And what was in her mind that was her own? That she wanted the girl to come down. To come down to her. To come down to her for her sake. For her own sake. She wanted the girl to come down for her own sake because she wanted to be with the girl. Yes, the girl had appeared at the right time. She had come exactly at the time the woman was considering becoming an animal.

"That's better," the girl said.

"How do you know? Why do you presume to know what I'm thinking?" the woman shouted into the leaves with as much wonder as irritation.

"I don't know exactly what you're thinking, only if you're thinking about me, about yourself or about something else. Sometimes I know more, sometimes I know the shape of your thinking. You were thinking about you. You were thinking about changing shapes. You were thinking about being a shapeshifter." The girl's tone had shifted to the murmur of kindly musing. Revealing herself as she was considering the woman. For the briefest moment, the woman could see the girl clearly. Girl, leaves, branches, sky, clouds were all distinct. The girl was not deliberately obfuscating the situation.

"You want to be someone else. You want to be like me."

Was this indeed true? Had the woman dared such a thought? Was she, herself, considering that such activities might be for her?

The girl laughed. "I just made that up. I don't ever really know what you're thinking."

"I think you do know what I'm thinking."

"I don't know a lot about thinking. It shifts too fast. Thinking doesn't have any substance to it. Do you know what I mean?"

"Do you ever lie?" The woman believed that the girl would answer this question truthfully and she thought she needed to know the answer.

"No."

What did the girl mean by such a no? The girl's answer implied that the question was unthinkable but not on moral grounds. To lie would be, the woman assumed the girl meant, unnatural, but the girl would not use such categories. The woman did use such categories and was constantly concerned with trying to discern the natural from the unnatural.

"You are going to give me a headache if you keep thinking so much. Your thoughts are like splatter shots, you follow one line and then you have to follow another. It's so arbitrary. You've got a brain," the girl said, "like a Jackson Pollack painting."

Then the woman remembered that among other things, the girl was a painter. And wasn't really a girl, only appeared so. Because of the delicacy of her bones and the openness of her face, her innocence. But she was far from innocent. Because she couldn't dissemble. Wouldn't dissemble. She appeared like a child because of her honesty. "I mean I don't ever really know for sure, what you are thinking."

The woman could not discern whether the girl didn't have the capacity to decipher her thoughts or whether her thoughts were confused and so were indecipherable.

"What I am thinking or what anyone is thinking?" the woman asked.

"What you are thinking."

"But I need to know just this," the woman tried to cajole a truthful answer, "would you ever say anything that was not true?"

"Do you mean like rabbits or doves making distress sounds away from their nests in order to distract the crows? That's not lying."

"What is it?"

"It's what they do. What small animals do."

She was, herself, very much a small animal, in that moment.

"What's a lie, then? Is a lie doing what you don't do? Are you a ... ?" the woman didn't know what word to follow with. "Are you someone who lies or someone who doesn't lie? And if you're someone who lies, is it lying when you lie?"

"Do you think I would lie to you?" The girl had nailed her. She didn't want to know if the girl lied, she didn't so much want to know the girl's nature, she wanted to know if the girl would lie to her. She wanted to know if they were having a relationship. If the girl cared that she, that she in particular, was sitting under the sycamore, waiting.

"Yes, of course I think that." Now the girl was forcing her to be truthful. "Am I right?"

"I don't lie."

'Why not?"

"I never have to."

"Are you lying?

The question was a triumph, but the woman couldn't maintain it and found herself asking immediately, "Would you like some juice? Or cookies?"

The girl did not answer and her silence was inevitable. It wasn't like the woman to resort to such pat maternal questions. The woman no longer knew whether the words that came out of her mouth were the result of her will or whether she had become some puppet, some marionette operated by a master puppeteer from a remote distance. How like the girl it would be to put words in her mouth and then jeer at them or take umbrage and retreat.

"Aren't you ready to come down?"

The woman waited, she heard nothing but the swish and click of leaves and branches. Then she roused herself to search for the girl who could not be seen and then the woman perceived that she was scrambling up higher and deeper into the tree where some vines, ivy and wisteria had woven a scaffolding. If it were earlier in the season when the wisteria vines that had entangled themselves about the branches were blooming like so many beaded curtains, like so many pale mauve clusters of grapes, they would have framed the girl and softened her retreat, without the girl needing to cloud the woman's mind.

She saw something. She could say it was the girl and certainly a physiological analysis would confirm it, but it was not the girl, not the girl she had been speaking with. It was another being. More shadowy and tentative.

It had lost the affirmation of its flesh and boundaries. Earlier it had exuded grief and now it exuded fear and fear existed in other dimensions altogether. Fear was not all together. Fear was in pieces and that was its disguise. The girl was in pieces and when the woman located her, she landed in between one part and another. She could not get a grip on the girl at all because the broken shards cut her mind. And just as she tried to withdraw her gaze and her desire, the sycamore, solid as sycamores are, was taken by an aspen-like tremor which crackled like lightning transmitted from the girl directly through the trunk into the woman. She was struck deeply. Now the woman knew fear in the manner of the girl.

"I'm sorry," she said simply. "I don't know what I did, but I'm sorry." But even as she said this, she knew it was hopeless. First of all it wasn't the same girl. Fear had altered the girl entirely so that she was now someone else. And so the words had no meaning as they were addressed to a different person and referred to something that had happened to that other being, to someone with whom she had had, she had hoped, to someone with whom she had once had a relationship. The object of her conversation had disappeared. This being in the tree was a total stranger, more foreign than monkey would have been, or wolf. Or the coyote for that matter. She was speaking to a creature who had manifested from the realization that the woman had tried to trick her.

Remorse overwhelmed her. There was nothing to be done. She might have to leave and abandon the girl to the firemen after all. The thought was more of a pout than an idea and she indulged this sulkiness, until an unusual movement startled her. Until the woman actually saw a wolf. Where the girl had been or was; it was difficult to tell which because the assemblage of girl was so mutable. Now you see her, now you don't.

Staring at the place where the girl had been until a second ago, the woman thought she was seeing her and then through her. As if the girl was transparent in the way a wave curving up for ten feet can appear transparent when it turns ice blue as the light penetrates it, the same color as secret caverns in banks of new fallen snow startled awake by sunlight. Then in the same moment, the girl had density to her, an obstinate and distinct mammalian density that seemed to imply bone, teeth, hide, fur.

Where the girl had been and still was, simultaneously, was a white wolf.

An arctic wolf, pure white, long legged, sleek and graceful. You could see right through it the way you could see right through the girl. In the way one could sometimes see through grief but could never see through fear. Yes. When you looked through it, it and the girl disappeared and what you saw was the void. That is, you saw what you couldn't see, what couldn't be seen. You saw that.

A shiver went through the woman that wasn't sent by the girl. A shiver of her own making and realization. She was looking at the wolf. The girl hadn't become a wolf so much as the woman was seeing a wolf. The woman was learning to see.

Folie á deux, she thought, before she could stop herself. She hoped the girl hadn't read these words in her mind. What a way to say thank you for this unexpected, unanticipated, unforeseen gift. She was being given the gift of seeing. Seer. As a child she had dreamed of seers, but she hadn't thought she could become one.

Squinting against the light, she followed the movement of the white wolf through the leaves. It climbed as gingerly as it might walk on ice. Exquisite the way it placed itself, the way it pulled all animal knowledge into its gestures, its paws delicate as the hooves of a newborn deer, its step certain as the mountain goat. It was going up. And up. She feared for it. For the fall. The tree shook, from the weight, she thought, of the large mammal clambering toward lighter crystalline branches of ice.

Apparently, the woman didn't know how to respond to this apparition any better than she had known how to treat the other one. She only knew that whenever she fell into the habit of returning in her mind to whatever she had known about the girl, trying to understand the girl, her motivations, these symptoms, the kind of traumas that might have brought her here, her fears and concerns, both of their fears and concerns, the trembling increased. The leaves of the tree chattered in the windless wind. Every random thought, every clutch toward strategy, every hope set the tree rocking in a hail storm.

"Stop shaking the damn tree, you're going to fall down." The woman called up hopefully.

"When the bough breaks, the cradle will fall, down will come, down will come, down will come, down will come...." It was a wisp of a song, almost an incantation, a small hope like a dandelion dissolving on the wind.

The woman watched the fluff of the dandelion, the precious cargo of seed, the robust tang of dark and bitter leaf allied with deep yellow flower encoded in so light a flight of possibility. There it went — hope, tomorrow, future — all floating away from her to find itself its own beginning elsewhere.

"Down will come baby, come baby, come baby, come baby," the woman sang too. A harmony created. They met on the common note and played there with each other, thoughtlessly. The tree stopped trembling. The wind sat still in the leaves like the sheen of light. It was exactly that time, that moment in late afternoon when light flares out onto the horizontal and is caught on the leaf and changes its color to variations of silver and gold. A peerage of light. Instead of the descent, of the light falling upon, there is a moment when the tree and the light meet each other for the enactment of the continuous exchange. The light meets the tree; the tree becomes enlightened and breathes out, so. The wolf threw back her head, raised her jaw, howled and disappeared.

"I'm yours," the woman sighed, as surprised by the words as by anything that had yet happened. Spreading her arms she threw herself back onto the ground. "I'm yours," she said again, meaning it, giggling. Happy.

Piss damp and muddy, thwarted in all possible ways, she had come to the only possible solution. She gave herself away. The idea delighted her but she was careful not to let it remain an idea. This was a challenge. She knew what she had to do. And was afraid that such knowing would undo her. She was to hold on to the delight while she let the idea escape from her. She couldn't do it and remain herself, that was clear. If she was herself she would inevitably think, she would think about what someone else had said about such moments in order to understand, she would take out the library card of her mind and rummage through files, she would turn on the internal world wide web. She would compare this moment with something she had already experienced, she would introduce memory or she would wonder if it would continue, she would introduce hope, anticipation, calculation.

No. Stop. She took a breath. Delight in and of itself. As brief and continuous as water. For a second she was water. She couldn't do it for long. Rain became stream and stream became lake and then the lake was dammed and so was she.

But until then, delight. Squirrel, she thought. Squirrel and delight are synonymous. The squirrel she was becoming in her mind ran up and down the tree, up and down the tree, up and down the tree, not going too close to the girl but close enough to display the rapture of fur and tail.

She opened her eyes wondering if squirrels ever tired, if squirrel ever thought about fatigue, if squirrel would say, "I should rest now." Finding these tedious questions, she searched out exactly the right place for squirrel to sequester herself, a little nook between trunk and branch, and found the girl, almost upside down, her face hanging down from the branch staring at her with curiosity. Then the woman thought, knowing she was thinking, knowing she was not yet able to avoid thinking, she thought, no she felt with certainty that the girl was looking at her with affection.

"That's very good," the girl said and settled into this niche which was closer to where she had been when the woman had first spotted her in the tree. The girl took out a handful of dried cranberries and tossed a few down to the woman before she put one, then a second, then a third into her mouth, sucking first and then as the cranberry softened chewing it ever so long. Savoring it.

"I didn't think you had it in you," the girl said.

"Had what in me? I'm trying to get rid of everything in me."

"Had nuts in you. I didn't think you had nuts in you."

"Nuts to you," the woman said, pleased with herself.

"We can stay here forever," the girl sighed contentedly.

"Hmm," the woman's heart was sinking. "What will we do?"

"I'll tell you stories."

"Aren't you uncomfortable?"

"Oh, no, I'm very comfortable. Look I can see in all directions. Oh, you can't see from there. Why don't you come up?" Had she forgotten that earlier she had warned the woman to stay below? "There's plenty of room. That's why I chose this sycamore. It has enough room for everyone.

"You'll have to learn to climb, you know."

"I think you should come down, first. You can't really be comfortable there." She paused. "I'm afraid of heights," she announced matter-of-factly. It was true. She had never spoken her fears thus. And, she had never spoken without thinking of what she going to say first. She used words with care. Words were her mojo. She was not casual in her use of language. She knew their effect. But now she had done it. The words had slipped out of her mouth. And it changed the arrangement between them. It wasn't only that she wanted the girl down. It was also that she was afraid of up.

"How can it be comfortable?"

"Quite comfortable. Really. This is my home."

"No. You have another home. Surely you do."

"No, not anymore."

Then the woman knew that the girl had definitively left the two women with whom she had been living. That this climb up the tree was not a temporary matter. That she was not in a pout. She was making her home here because it was the best of the options that were available to her.

"You have another place," the woman said without knowing, once again, what she was saying. "You have a place with me." The words were spoken before she understood them herself. She repeated them, this time thinking of what the words meant, then saying them carefully so she would not be misunderstood, and so carefully that she, herself, would understand what she was saying. "You have a place with me." Then she picked up the socks the girl had dropped and folded them neatly into one of the shoes and aligned them by the trunk, experiencing a maternal confidence she had never known.

"I once had another place," the girl said. "It was a long time ago."

The woman waited. Out of respect for the girl, she attempted a common language. She tried to breathe the way elk breathe, the way rabbits breathe, without betraying their presence. She took long, slow, deep breaths as if she was taking in the tree, the light, the clouds that were passing overhead, even the girl. She could hear the girl's breath exit from her mouth and she took it in then let it go herself when she thought the girl was ready to receive it. It went on a long time, this breathing.

She didn't know how long they sat this way, silently together. So long that she didn't realize the girl was speaking until she was far into the story. She didn't know when this occurred and she didn't know where. The girl was saying that she had seen snow bears coming at dusk to hot springs in the snow river and that she had followed them closely. The girl must have been very explicit, because the woman imagined it so exactly, she thought it was occurring around her though clearly there were no hot springs nor a snow river in the tree.

Still, as if it were happening, as if she were entirely submerged in the girl's memory or imagination, she saw the girl getting down on her hands and feet, one arm outstretched and then the leg following it swaying from side to side, careful to display her spreading fingers and toes to the bears, not to disturb them with her foreignness as she made her way down to the roiling waters. Without changing her posture or rather the rhythm of it, the girl rolled out of the clothes she had worn to the snow river, though the woman was aware that she was also, simultaneously naked in the tree, and let her hair fall down her back, was entirely covered by her own mane and so pungent with the sweat from her effort and the additional sweat of apprehension and some moisture of fear and the various odors of excitement, that the bears had allowed her to crawl onto the large flat rock that was both pedestal and platform and dangle her feet into the water. Then in bear time, they found her sufficiently familiar and harmless enough to let her slip entirely into the warm rapids where she, bear, stone, all smelled equally of the purity of sulfur and could be said to have become kin.

"How many bears?" the woman asked, so focused on the girl, she couldn't see the other animals clearly.

The girl was trying to remember, she was counting. Big Momma on the same pedestal. Big Poppa up there on the rocky wall cascading directly into the river. Big Momma's three sisters, two older sons, two older daughters, the three babies ... twelve.

"I was the thirteenth. They fed me snow berries and snow apples. I made them garlands for their hair."

"Did they like them?"

"After Big Momma put hers on they all wanted garlands of honeysuckle. Later they made them themselves and wove them about each other."

"It's not true." It was a stupid response, but the woman couldn't prevent herself from uttering it.

"It's true. I was with them in the snow river, in the mountains. You can

29

only go there in winter when the hot springs melt the ice over the river."

"There are no honeysuckles in winter." Why was she persisting in this way?

The girl, however, was not dismayed. "You should see what grows along the snow banks of the hot springs where no one goes in the winter. You should see what grows where no one is but the snow bears and the steam spirits. That kind of honeysuckle only grows in moonlight. They need silver light to grow. The vines wrap themselves around the wine blood leaves of the plum tree. They are the arms of Pachamama. You should see it. I'll take you some day. You'll have to grow your hair long though. They won't let you in otherwise. You have to grow your hair down to your mid-back. They will love you because your hair is silver like the moonlight. You will look like the silverback bear that appears only once in two generations."

"Why do you tell me such things?"

"Because you love the beautiful," she said.

"And where did you learn about the beautiful?"

"From the snow bears. They taught me."

The words repeated in the woman's mind not like a thought but like a liturgy or an invocation. "Because you love the beautiful."

The afternoon light crept down the tree and illuminated the girl's face. She was like a sunflower. She turned, as if she knew what the woman was seeing, full face into the light, the way sunflowers turn, fields of them in exact rows, six feet high all of them, facing into the sun.

Then she knew something she couldn't stand knowing. She was beginning to love the girl. And because of this, she was being called out of time. She was nowhere. That is, she was nowhere she had ever been before. Or she was everywhere. The words echoed in her chest even when she didn't understand them. There were words inside of her that she didn't understand and they weren't someone else's words.

"This is a serious business," the woman confided to the girl after some time had gone by. How much time? A half dozen cranberries had gone by. It was an interesting measure both precise and imprecise at the same time.

Faintly, she understood that the girl was teaching her something that she had recently hoped to learn but without any hope of it ever being accomplished. It was a glimpse she was being given. Only a glimpse. But it was enough to be willing to become a student.

She was becoming aware of the great difference between her and the girl. The girl was the girl, entirely herself, clear as water. While she, the woman, was besieged by a dozen different voices, by ideas of what was or wasn't or should or shouldn't be, by theories and assumptions, that did not want to allow her to take the girl — she was naked in the tree — seriously. So not knowing how to respond, what to do that was sensible in response to the girl, she allowed herself to review what she knew about animals. And that being a short file, she let herself ruminate on why she didn't know much about animals. Seemingly the girl had no objection to these considerations, she didn't change her position in the tree, she didn't start climbing away and the leaves weren't trembling. The light was leaving the sky and catching on the leaves.

How had she come here? the woman wondered.

Now the woman became aware that she was caught in an impossible dilemma. She could either "save" the girl against her will, give it a try that is, or let the girl save her by allowing herself to become an animal. Suddenly not being certain of who needed to be saved was causing mental dizziness. This was not going to be easy. Becoming an animal was certainly not going to be easy. It was not something one fell into in the ways one fell so easily into sin, fell prey to sin, or so radio and TV ministers claimed, as if all one had to do was to perch oneself atop a water slide in an amusement park designed for the purpose of the fall. And then let go. Being an animal was not hovering dangerously at the bottom of any slide waving its ragged tail, showing its long teeth, blowing fetid breath.

"Don't eat that way," her mother had always cautioned her, "do you think you're an animal?" Or, "Say please so people won't think you're an animal." Or, "Clean your room, you're living like an animal. Close the door, do you think we live in a barn?" Over a period of time the allusions became more specific. As her parents entered enthusiastically into the science of taxonomy, she was warned about being catty or piggish, being a vrona — that is spilling food out of her mouth as the story of the crow had it — making monkey faces, being a silly goat, becoming a horse's ass, a sheep led to the slaughter, a toad, a worm, a mule, a vixen, and then a hellhound. After the war, her father reverted to simplicities. He said the enemy were beasts. In any case, it wasn't as easy as her mother had said. Though she had not avoided all of the pitfalls, she had grown up into a very nice specimen of homo sapiens, thank you very much.

Damn the girl, she thought, and began to slip through the books she had herself read, reviewing what she knew. What she knew from ... fairy tales. Not a bad start. In these tales, someone was always turned into an animal by someone else. But it was a momentary euphoria because she soon remembered that the metamorphosis was only a question of appearances. Underneath the donkey skin, bird wing, bear pelt, astonished frog eyes was someone desperately trying to become human again. A human heart with all its contradictions, that commodity of humanity continued beating, lamenting under its disguise. To make matters worse, though human could not be entirely subsumed, this did not make the hybrid more attractive or less dangerous. Involuntary as the transformation was, the "debased" (according to the stories) animal nature prevailed; that was the hybrid's torture. The individuals had fallen into the evil hands of sorcerers or were being punished for some infractions by enchantresses, but one way or another, the transformations were against their will.

Enchantment, as enchanting as the word was, implied domination. The sorcerer dominated his victim as surely as the animal nature dominated the human and one quickly found oneself in hell. The way out was precarious. Confined as one was within the animal, one had to find one's way back to one's angelic nature or had to engage someone else's spiritual power, in order to shed this inhibiting skin. The story, ultimately was not about becoming an animal, it was about the means of return. And if one decided to stay, well then one was a werewolf. And that was the worst of all, wasn't it?

This was not the woman's idea of becoming an animal. And even if she were willing to risk living out the story the way it had been told over and over again for the sake of attempting a takeover of the animal's exalted nature and remaining in that condition, or learning how to travel from one form to another, she didn't know a local ogre, witch or sorcerer whom she could entice into helping her exchange one set of DNA for another.

In retrospect, she realized she hadn't ever been instructed in the ways of animals let alone becoming one. Born into another culture she might have been initiated into such mysteries. The only mystery her mother alluded to was why, when she had been a girl, she had insisted on sleeping with her dog. This, her mother said was a great mystery.

Leaning against the tree, having settled in, if necessary, for the night, with this flower of a wolf child blooming above, alternately howling or singing or moaning like a magnolia waiting to burst open into evening perfumes, purple at the stem where branch and bloom bled into each other, she remembered the moment she had deliberately forgotten that there had been different peoples that believed special ones could change themselves into animals. Perhaps there still were such people. She had not known then, and perhaps did not know yet, that these ones who could make these changes, who would consider such a transmutation, had to know the nature of the animal as well as they understood their own nature. Otherwise they would become mutants, monsters, undeveloped abominations with open sores such as wandered the world everywhere in human form because the entity, ignorant of its own nature when it took it on, went about in its own distortion.

The girl howled again, out of exuberance this time, not fear. Howled and listened and howled again and listened. From the distance, an answer. Which neighborhood dog, the woman wondered, trying to identify it. Then she cocked her head, the way the girl was cocking her head, and held her breath the way the girl was holding her breath and turned slowly as if directing the antennas of her ears, the way the girl was pivoting, listening as carefully as she thought the girl was listening and in this way she recognized the call. Her own wolf. From several miles away the way the crow flies. Timber.

"You know that I live with a wolf." She had not wanted to play all her cards. She had been saving this one ever since she had been trying to determine the girl's genetic pattern.

"I knew that before I ever came to visit you. I wouldn't have come otherwise." She howled then, exquisitely, plaintively, eloquently. The howl took the woman in the same way she had sometimes been pierced and penetrated by a flute, the sound curved through the woman's body like the breaking of a wave and then again and again. Such a sound, she thought, can conjure the moon. Then Timber answered.

How had she come to this place? she asked herself. Her people had a sacred prayer that she had taken for herself: "Thank you for bringing me to this place." She never went to services but she had come upon this prayer and took to saying it again and again. Sometimes several times a day. It was like a window. She would say the prayer and then it was as if shutters opened and a window appeared which was clean, gleaming, perfectly transparent, and she could see. Out. Watch out.

She heard herself saying the prayer under her breath even though she didn't know why she was saying it nor why she was here She had, apparently been saying it for a long time. Her own behavior was more mysterious to her than the girl's behavior.

At first, it had been easy to explain. She was here for the girl. She was acting therapeutically. But that excuse had disappeared in the last few hours. She was here for her own sake. The girl was incidental, was the excuse, was the guide and the core of why she was here. But she was here for herself.

How had she come to this place? Not knowing how to answer this question, she thought she'd start at the beginning, put the first memories at one end and this event at the other end in order to fill in the middle. Between the two points was a mysterious line; some events would fit on the line and some wouldn't. All roads would lead from the first place to the last place as these were the roads of her life but still there was one line which was most direct or inevitable or ... beautiful.

She had been born at the seashore. This was the saving grace — and the woman did mean Grace — of her life. She had been born from one internal sea in her mother's womb into another sea, had known salt water, inner and outer, from the very beginning. To live by the sea which she had done until she was in her twenties was to live in beginnings. The woman was delighting in her own musings. She had never heard her story told this way. She had never told it to herself. In all the years she had spent listening to people's stories, she had never heard this story which was her own.

Almost before she had entered into the story, she found herself thinking about other stories, others' stories, repeating them in her mind. Then she began wondering if she had listened attentively enough to the girl's story, if she had fastened on to the right details, if ... dead end. The woman returned to her own story.

Recently, the woman had watched a whale and dolphins surface and dive, surface and dive. It was not that they were going to their roots, they were going beyond roots, they were going to the salty place of primordial form. To the ooze. Dipping down into creation itself and then leaping into the air, ecstatic, half turn, flip, flip, and the dolphins, two, three, four, were down again as the whale came up so slowly, you couldn't believe that it would rise so, like a mountain in the midst of its own creation, and then settle back, an island sinking into the beginning again.

She had been standing on the balcony of a rented beachside house on the Big Island, Hawaii, watching dolphins cavort and a whale and her calf, rise and fall, rise and fall. Each day. For several days. At the same time, two in the afternoon, in the same place. And she remembered this: the event had filled her with unexpected grief, unbearable sadness which she had never fathomed. The woman remembered how she had, from childhood, watched the waves, watched the tides, watched fish, dolphins, whales, gulls, terns, pelicans, moon rise and sun set.

That is how she got here. She had started at the beginning. She had not bypassed anything essential. She had studied the essentials. She had never told her story this way before and she liked this story. She wondered what the girl thought of the story, how she read it, how it appeared to the girl as she perused the woman's mind.

It was simple. Simple in the way she could sense salt in the air when the wind changes and comes in from the gray sea. The way she sometimes smelled roses one moment and seaweed the next and seaweed was the winner, became the beloved. She would set out toward kelp without even realizing she had stepped out of the garden gate and was heading down to the jetty.

She had spent her girlhood on deserted beaches, at the bay, meandering about through the flotsam and jetsam thrown up by storms. She would wander through the skeleton of a hospital ship which had beached in the early years of the war. She would call to the gulls. She had stayed at the water's edge during storms. She had dared lightning. She had gone into the ocean secretly when no one was about in late autumn and early spring. She had skittered out on the small reefs of ice during the winter. She had dreamed of polar bears as lovers.

"I was born by the sea," she said. "That's the true story," she told the girl. "I was born by the sea. I loved sailors. I picked them up in the city and brought them home and fed them roast beef sandwiches and potato salad. God knows what my mother thought of all of this. Then I would ask them for their stories. They wanted to tell me about girls and foreign ports and battles; I wanted to know about sea birds and sea mammals. I wanted to know what they had seen, how it had changed them. I wanted to slither in the water with them, but it was prohibited. So I pulled out the hook and threw them back."

Was she committing a gross indiscretion by telling the girl this? How old was the girl anyway? There was no way to tell. She could have been fourteen. She could have been forty. The woman felt that the girl knew about such states of mind, she might have coupled with mermen.

"Would you prefer me not to say anything about this?"

"Please tell it all. It's so much harder for me to have to read your mind precisely. I get it confused with my mind and all the colors run, blue and red, into purple and on and on and on."

"I wanted the sailors to tell me about the sea. I didn't care where they landed. I wasn't interested in where they had been. I wanted to stand at the shoreline with them and have them tell me what it was like to be in the very center of the salty endlessness. In the way the world is divided, in the ways some of us choose sugar and some of us choose salt, count me as one of the salt people."

The girl showed her teeth as a way of acknowledging a certain fierceness in the woman. The fierceness of salt, an attribute she could trust. The girl showed her teeth again but differently this time.

She inclined her body toward the woman as if to whisper in her ear though they were quite a distance apart. "For myself," she confided, "I would like to have my teeth carved. I would like to find an old Inuit man who has spent his life carving balls of bone and tusk rolling around inside balls of bone rolling inside balls of ivory bone and ask him to teach me how to carve. Like spider webs inside spider webs inside spider webs. Then I will carve my own teeth." She would do scrimshaws on her own teeth in the way she took octopus ink and painted whirling suns, the arrows of rain, feathers, meanders of nightfall across her cheekbones. The girl wanted that work done on her eye teeth, first, on her fangs. "So that when I bare my teeth, everyone will be afraid." In the moment, she contented herself with showing her teeth in such a way that the woman could, if she were willing, and she was more than willing, see the carving, years of handiwork on whale bone, could see the years of sailing back and sailing back and sailing back or north and then north and then north.

"Frio," the girl said.

"Who's that?"

"My white wolf."

"You have a wolf?"

"Yes. But she's not here yet. She's coming." The gash of her mouth. Not a smile but an opening of the mouth, lips opened and pressed flat back so that as much of the teeth as was possible were displayed. Yah! There. As firm and economical a gesture as if she had bitten down hard once on the woman's hand and held there. Rrrruh. No sound but if there had been a sound it would have been an opened mouthed Hss to begin with. The Yah from the rush of breath across the young girl's palette, and the growl, grrr, from the curve of the breath in the little granite cave behind the small, white, even teeth as they fastened down.

She was bitten. Her hand in the wolf's mouth. Muzzle closing. Saliva. The woman watched it happen to her. Feral was the word she used to explain the girl and what the girl was doing to her. Feral. It was efficient. Feral. Again. Good. The woman liked the girl better and better.

The girl leaned forward even more, growling. The woman heard the growl but she couldn't keep her mind on it. Awkwardly, the woman had begun to travel as the girl traveled so easily. She found herself in her own territory, in a whale, traveling up her bones, carving her initials on the white matter. The belly of the whale was a comfortable seat. She settled into it. Stretched out her legs, took in the odors of plankton, sea water. She felt the whale's weighty grace. Oh, hold on, we are going up! She held on to the ribs, a long boat going up, up, up. A Coney Island ride. Steeplechase. The roller coaster. Up, up, only to go down, going down, going down fast.

The girl had stopped growling and was staring at the women with wonder. "You know how to sit still," she marveled. "Where did you go?"

"Whales," the woman said.

"I was thinking about arctic wolves and ice flows," the girl responded.

Peering down at the woman as she settled back against the trunk as if she really knew how to sit under a tree for a long time, the girl recognized that the woman was no longer impatient. But the girl saw the unuttered word, feral, still hovering in the woman's imagination. The girl looked at her hands and the woman followed her scrutiny. They were not paws. They were exquisitely agile. The girl had been born with the opposing thumb of opposing thumbs. She was an artist. She would carve her own teeth more delicately than any scrimshaw.

Feral took the girl. She fell into the animal. The north. Snows she had never seen. Glaciers so blue they were emerald green. All the time it was happening, the woman saw it happening. The entire world of snow colors, variations on night blindness whirled within her, about her. The woman shuddered with cold. And awe. Wolf. Girl. Frio. Who could tell them apart?

Fact? Fact of nature. Indisputable. There had been peoples who could turn themselves into animals. Fact? Did they still exist? Unlikely. But there were records, weren't there? Perhaps. Of a certain kind. Hermetic records. Sealed until this moment from the likes of her. That wasn't important. What was important were the facts, not speculations. She was not thinking of werewolves or vampires.

Did they still exist?

Unlikely.

Unlikely? Was she thinking unlikely even when she might be in the presence of one? Was she blind? Deaf? A fool?

Her mind teetered. She couldn't encompass what she had just understood. To escape the certain knowledge that dizzied her so much more than the whale ride, she went on into the vertigo and the sanctuary of her mind.

There had been animals that could turn themselves into people. Fact?

She was happier with the first piece of knowledge than she was with the second. But she realized this in time because the first piece of knowledge was definitely about to vanish without the company of the second piece of knowledge. She had no control over any of this, not even, unfortunately, what her mind could absorb.

There had also been animals that could turn themselves into people. Fact?

Did she know it? Did she know it yet? She was coming to know it. She could feel the knowledge coming into her. Actually it wasn't like that. It wasn't like drinking a potion. It wasn't like eating. It was something else. What was it?

Once she was knowing what she was coming to know, an entire world was constellating itself around her. There were consequences to this knowledge. She was elsewhere. Elsewhere had other postulates and laws. One derived from another. If people turned themselves into animals then animals turned themselves into people. If one was true, the other was true. Axiomatic. She was indeed, entering another world altogether. An other world very much all together.

Momentarily, she forgot the girl except as a comforting presence who would be attended later. The girl was safe. As long as she was in the tree, she was safe. Even though wolves didn't usually make trees their habitat. She thought that thought again: As long as the girl was in the tree, she was completely safe, secured, looked after.

With that thought, the woman had crossed over yet another singularity. The woman followed the path of this thought as it streaked through her mind like those occasional streaks of lightning that travel horizontally, going elsewhere.

She forced her mind away from the girl and what the girl had just taught her, back to the animals. She knew that knowledge gained and not integrated was dangerous. Two things could happen; the first was the worst. The knowledge having finally come — back — that was the crucial word. The knowledge having finally come back could disappear forever if it were not taken in fully and respectfully. A second disappearance did not auger a second return. The second possibility would be that she would absorb it defectively, would only half take it in, would distort it to accommodate her past experience or the various dominant traditions that agreed only in their opposition to this knowledge. Or she would tuck it away like an exotic plant that lived in a pot in a dark stairwell, watered daily, lit by a specially devised fluorescent type grow bulb and sprayed occasionally with a faint mist expelled from a red nozzle on a white opaque plastic bottle.

She took in the thought and repeated it clearly, searched her pockets for a piece of paper and a pen which she always carried with her but had left in her purse in the car. She was not going to violate this moment by getting up and looking for them. And, anyway, knowledge was coming too fast. Far too fast.

She imagined herself speaking to the wolf, Timber: "Timber, please transmit more slowly so I can write down what you're thinking." She would simply work at remembering even though remembering was not one of her talents. She would work at it.

She returned to the thought at hand and repeated it several times. There were or had been animals who deliberately changed themselves into humans. Then the thought developed and it made her dizzy but she simply pressed her head hard into the trunk of the tree and moved it around until she found a burl that she could scratch her horns against to keep herself alert: There were or had been animals who deliberately and consciously changed themselves into humans, other animals, plants or elementals. This took her to another impossible conception: animals, plants, elementals, humans, stones, they were possibly, under some conditions, interchangeable. She couldn't state it the way she understood it but she knew she knew something.

Could it, whatever it was she knew now, be true?

She glanced up at the girl, furtively.

It was true.

It was too complicated for her. The truth of it made her dizzy and dull. She went back to the first thought. There were or had been animals who deliberately and consciously changed themselves into humans just as there had been humans who had for similar reasons changed themselves into animals.

Fact.

A girl who had suffered from anorexia had confessed to the woman that she had been so crazed that she would only eat dog food from the dog's bowl and her father fed her that way. "You live like an animal," her father

41

had said, "eat like an animal," and he had thrust the damned bowl onto the floor and watched only a moment while she got up from the corner of the room where she had been curled and crawled on her hands and knees to the bowl and began licking the food. Licks being all that she allowed herself.

This was not what the woman now meant by becoming an animal. This was the degradation of the animal. That is what the anorexic girl had been enacting. She had been so clever, no one, certainly not her father had understood that she was doing whatever she could to kill the animal inside of her.

The only thing that could bring the hungry girl to such a desperate condition was pain. The woman had seen such cases many times. The pain was so pervasive, there was only one possible response to it: Kill!

If I could become an animal, the woman was thinking, if I could become a bird, I could fly.

She remembered something. A different kind of remembering. She remembered it from books. It was said that the peoples who could turn themselves into animals believed that the gods also came to earth in the shape of animals. There were two beliefs that she had read. That some gods were always in the shapes of animals and some gods took on the shapes of animals on different occasions.

She took in the consequences of this memory and was grateful that she was not being required to absorb it into her consciousness. Fact? Fact that she remembered reading it.

The woman looked up at the girl in the tree or rather she looked up at the white wolf that hovered about the girl like a radiant mist and she promised herself she would enter the long and meticulous practice of separating the degradation of the animal from the annunciation of the animal, now that she had found her sorceress.

"I'll make you a deal," the woman said. "You come down from the tree and I'll apprentice myself to you. You get room and board and I get a teacher."

"But why should I come down from the tree?"

"Because my back hurts," the woman offered. "And I'm hungry. And, if you must know as I don't have fur, there's a chill entering my ass and traveling up my spine."

'You go so far and then you go back," the girl noted.

"If I were a bird..." the woman responded feebly.

"I don't think you're trustworthy. You have the moral fiber of a social worker." It was clear the girl wasn't impressed by the woman's explanations. Her face pursed as if it had bitten an unripe fruit and the matted tang sent shivers through her. "You're the dog catcher, that's who you are. You would use anything, you would even use a bear trap. Ahuuuu." She had kept the pucker and raised her mouth to the moon that was rising and let go with another howl exquisite enough to convince the woman that the girl had learned it sometime in her life from the real thing.

"You know," the woman said, standing up and brushing the earth off her jeans, "I think I'm trustworthy. I wouldn't have said that earlier but I think it's true now."

"You think too much," the girl said.

"Still, I feel trustworthy."

"Where do you feel it?"

She didn't know and trying several locations settled on putting her arms out as if holding a huge clay pot. Then unable to find the exact location of trust in her torso, she picked up a cookie. The gesture, of course, startled the girl who began to scamper up the tree.

"The cookies are poisoned," the girl cautioned in a voice subdued by terror.

"I doubt it. But if you think so, wait to see if I die before you eat any of them. On the other hand, they may be all gone by the time you think they're safe. I'm hungry myself. I could cook us a meal at home. It's been a very long day. Longer for you, I think, but long enough.

"There's a tree at my house," she continued believing that she would convince the girl if she could say everything without being interrupted. Bombardment was her current ploy. "I don't know if you noticed it when you came to visit me. It's a pepper tree, quite sturdy and except for the hornets in summer, you'll find it to your liking. Several large branches meet near the top — they'll hold you — and from there you can probably see 360 degrees, even along the canyon that leads in from the sea. Do you play the flute? I haven't tried it myself. It's a good tree for flutes."

"How will I live?" the girl asked.

"There's a trailer behind the white oleander bushes. It was just vacated. A woman artist was living there. She left for the southwest. She found the area too civilized. As you will too, no doubt. She left her stone carving tools. Interested?"

"What do you do for a living?" the girl asked.

"I train dolphins to jump out of the water, do a double somersault and grab fish out of my hand."

"Do you really?" The girl was not impressed.

"Of course not."

"What then?"

"You remember. You came to see me once. People tell me their stories and it makes them happy."

"Really?"

"Sometimes. Sometimes they remain miserable."

"What else?"

"Sometimes I tell people stories."

"And then?"

"And then they're happy or sad."

"Really?"

"Really."

"I would like to do that but I don't like people very much."

"No, I don't imagine you do. Why should you? They aren't very likable as a rule."

"Will you tell me stories?" In the middle of the question the girl became quite small, so small that the woman remembered Lewis Carroll and realized that he must have watched similar transformations. The girl who had been thirteen or fourteen at the least was now about three years old.

The woman was aware that the alteration had happened in an instant but at the same time she had witnessed the smooth progression backwards in precise detail.

This unusual event and the nature of the question silenced the woman. It was not a simple event and it was not a simple question. In addition, everything teetered on the answer. A domino effect was inevitable. The girl coming down from the tree. The girl finding a home....the girl.... Who knew what might happen after that.

Also the woman would never be the same. Nor her life. She could see her future laid out before her like a spread of cards and suddenly an invisible hand was gathering up the cards she'd been studying, which she had come to know over the years, love even, and was shuffling them back into the deck and laying them out again so that she recognized none of them nor the order they were in. A wind was coming up and blowing down the house of cards just as Carroll had predicted.

"Will you tell me stories?"

"I will tell you stories," she said as if she were being asked to swear an oath.

And so the girl belonged to her. She had wooed her. And she had won her. However, that is not the way the girl told the story afterwards. Later the girl implied that was the way the girl had won the woman, had won the woman over to her side.

"Do you really have a flute?" the girl whispered hopefully in a voice that sounded as if it had never before dared hope.

"A wooden flute. An alto recorder. I don't know how good it is. It was good once. It belonged to someone who died."

"She stopped playing the flute. Was that why she died?" the girl asked in a tremulous voice that remained almost inaudible whether — the woman couldn't decide which — it was modulated by fear or awe.

The girl's insight was stunning. The death had occurred ten years ago and the woman had never understood this simple fact. She did not deny the girl her understanding. "Yes, that is why she died," she said, nodding her head more to herself than to the girl. "I never thought of that before." The woman realized the girl, up in the tree, understood what she, the woman, was incapable of understanding from her vantage point below. "I've considered the reasons for her death every day for ten years," the woman was filled with sadness and rallied by adding, "though assuming that I understood it perfectly."

"You didn't know about the flute and so you didn't take good care of it. Is that right? You threw it in a basket with noisemakers, didn't you?"

As if to startle the woman further, the girl began to play the Jew's harp, a sad tune to meet the woman's sorrow, compelling her to be honest.

"Well, yes, I did. How do you know?"

"I saw it when Carmela brought me to visit you."

"And what did you think?"

"I thought I'm not going to tell this woman my story. She doesn't know anything but she thinks she does. She doesn't understand flutes."

"Will you come down now?"

There was a loud thump as something landed just beside the woman's feet. "Too bad you don't have coconuts," the woman sputtered as she jumped up, then belatedly to the side.

"I have whatever I need." The girl had thrown down her knapsack of treasures wrapped in her white T-shirts.

From another tree, they heard the call of a dove, a tremulous coo that pierced the last afternoon light with its own heartrending shimmer.

"I have seen the doves who paint their faces blue. They have pale blue circles around their eyes and soft blue cheek feathers," the girl said and pouted. From her pursed lips she uttered an answering coo that was exact in its call and lament.

Then she started coming down but not as the woman, who was standing and looking up expectantly, thought she would. Rising up onto her feet and hands so that all four were on a branch that could not possibly hold her, she walked down rump raised, baboon fashion until she was just above the woman's head and there she froze.

The recurrence of fear, however, the reflex of it, overwhelmed the girl's exquisite sense of balance and engineering and she was out on the prover-bial limb that suddenly didn't hold her and before the woman could scream, "Oh no," she was upon her and in the arms that had, it seemed, been proffered and they were both on the ground, the girl whimpering in the woman's arms and the woman nuzzling her and making unintelligible sounds which were, nevertheless, or, especially, comforting. And never having had children of her own, she found herself feeling more cow, horse, dog, bear than human, wanting to lick the girl all over, cleaning the dust and pebbles from her bruised cheek, with a long nappy tongue.

Instead she asked, "Did you break anything?"

"Did you?"

"I don't think so."

"Thinking won't tell you anything. Can you feel something broken?"

"No, I don't feel anything broken."

"Don't worry then."

"You don't worry either, then." Breathing was a little difficult after the fall. She waited until she could speak without gasping. "I still feel trust-worthy. Here," she said, meaning all of her, now that the girl was in her arms.

"Where's the food?" the girl asked. "Did you fall on it?"

"I'd be complaining, you can be sure, if I had. It's over there on the other side of the tree."

The girl bit each slice of fruit leaving a round indentation which she inspected and then nibbled at carefully so that the semi-circle was exact and aesthetically pleasing. She ate one of the hot dogs and then another and then took a bun and crumbled it carefully between her palms as if kneading clay into a cylinder and dropped the crumbs in a circle around the base of a neighboring eucalyptus. "The doves like to sit in this tree and look around. The crumbs are for them, but the jays will probably get them first. The doves are very shy, it has taken me months to get them to take the seeds I put out for them. First they wouldn't even come to the tree, then they wouldn't fly down from it."

The woman felt the shift in the girl as dramatic as a change in weather. And she responded as she might to clouds dispersing and sunshine appearing, to sudden warmth; she opened to it. She would have taken off her clothes in homage if she didn't think that the presence of another naked person would startle the already naked girl.

When the girl realized she hadn't offered the woman any food, she held the plate out sheepishly. "I thought you had eaten."

"It doesn't matter."

"Do you want some?"

"Don't you want the rest?"

"I want to leave some food for the raccoons and coyotes. Carmela says they're nuisances. 'Pests,' she calls them. 'Vermin.' So I have to feed them when she's not around. I'll have to come back here to feed them. You'll bring me back won't you? They're used to the food. They depend on it. And they won't know to follow me to your house. You will, won't you?"

"I will."

The girl took the rest of the food to the edge of the property where the grass met the scrub and put tiny pieces of bread and hot dog around the sage brush, far more content to offer them to the animals than to the woman. Even from a distance, the woman could see how carefully she did this, how meticulous she was in serving the animals who had been, so it seemed, her only reliable companions.

Then the girl walked naked, except for the knife in the sheath, but with a posture that implied clothing, to the car and crawled onto the back seat, curled up with her head on her paws so that by the time the woman got home, the girl was asleep.

The woman elected to sit by her in the car for several hours with the girl's head in her lap. The door to the woman's cottage was only a few steps away. She didn't go in. Instead she sat down on the back seat, lifted the girl's head gently, placing it on her lap, feeling the girl's dark hair cascading like skeins of heavy silk across her hands, then covering the girl with a mohair blanket she kept in the car. Intermittently, she thought of undoing the belt around the girl's waist or slipping the knife out of the sheaf, but she put those thoughts out of her mind. Better to remove the knife from her mind. Whatever reasonable explanation she gave herself, the truth was that she didn't want the girl to disappear. She didn't want her to awaken in anger or fear and so shapeshift into a bird and fly away. The girl might become anything, go anywhere, do anything. The woman … the woman… the woman wanted to go with her.

Only once did the woman allow professional thoughts to disturb the exquisite peace that existed between them. If someone came by… if she were discovered sitting with a naked girl in her lap… if she as a therapist were discovered with her naked client…if, on awakening, the girl had thought she might have abused her… if….

If can be a dangerous word, she contended to herself, trying to banish it from her mind. She focused on the stars, on the coyotes howling in the hills, on the entire animal valley suddenly alerted. Somewhere in the brush, Timber Wolf added his glorious arpeggio to the chorus. A conversation in progress that the woman had never thought to understand. As the girl was asleep, she took the opportunity to apply herself but the stars remained silent, the wolves, dogs and coyote's language was incomprehensible to her, and the night birds only sang their odd melodies intermittently. Failing to comprehend, the woman was unable to avoid the camber of her own thoughts.

She didn't know what her responsibilities were nor could she distinguish them from her inclinations, whatever they were. Everything was unfamiliar and unpredictable. She wanted to go with the girl and converted this, immediately, into ways she could entice the girl to stay with her. An about-face in her mind pretending not to be an about-face. A reassertion of a very different mind. A mind not unlike Carmela's mind, certain, self-righteous, determined. A different kind of shapeshifting altogether. More like possession, a thought, the kind of thought the girl might have had, flickered briefly through her consciousness, an ember quickly extinguished as the woman sank into the mindset of a strategist, not Carmela's mind, but her own old mind, very familiar and, yes, treacherous. She was unnerved and alternately was blaming the girl, Carmela, her peers, her profession. Such habits of mind often afflicted her clients. She was skilled at helping them because she knew the pattern and so could confront herself; it was not right to blame others for her face in her mirror.

They were at a crossroads. If getting the girl down from the tree seemed difficult, the next step, getting the girl into the house seemed even more daunting. There was no reason to think the girl would follow the woman anywhere. Even if she waited for the girl to awaken and then walked in the door of her house the way she always did, the girl would not follow her. She knew this. And if she followed the girl, the house would transform before them, would become in that instance, the girl's house, and she, the woman, would be nowhere, would have nothing of her own. She was as stubborn, it seemed, as the girl. She also was disinclined to follow. Was equally afraid of the ramifications.

In the park, a distant scream, no less wild and feline. It was true, then, there was a cougar in the territory. Good thing, then, that she had brought the girl home. "I am just waiting for the girl to awaken," that's what she told herself. "That's why I'm staying here," she told herself as she continued to stroke the girl's forehead, her shiny, irregularly cut, hacked, to be precise, black hair. Hair that wasn't familiar to the woman from her own family and kin. Had she been invited to cut it off, she would have saved it and braided it. It was smooth, abundant, straight as the razor the girl must have used to slice it off. At another time, the woman would have hacked off her own hair if it had been soaked with urine. She hadn't forgotten about it, she was discovering that she didn't care. In truth, it was very pleasant sitting in the back of her own car, both doors open, a spring night breeze coming in, the beginning of fog creeping up the hills toward the house which was perched like a lookout on a hill at the top of the canyon. In truth, she was as happy as she had ever been. In truth, she was already thinking that she loved the girl. In truth, she was wondering for the first time in her life what it would be like to have a child. In truth, she was imagining, not for the first time, what it might be like to live in truth.

In these night hours, the woman had time to reflect on her life. She recognized that she had always sought out those who would challenge her and open the door to new ways of living. The shelter that she was thinking would serve the girl, had belonged to a woman artist, V, who had lived on the woman's land and left the trailer behind. The artist who had happily spent three years living out of her car in remote, uninhabited reaches of the Malibu hills, must have spent nights like this when the chill or the heat enticed her to seek shelter. She had shown the woman the way she had arranged her car, portioning off places she called kitchen table and writing desk, painting studio, pantry, closet, library. Outside the car, she had made a shelter with four poles and a piece of pale blue silk she had dyed herself to resemble weather. In the rainy season, she had said, she would put a tarp over the poles, but otherwise she liked the illusion of shelter, not the fact of it. "The only real safety," she had insisted, "is under the stars."

What did she mean by that? The artist and the woman had exchanged many sentences, but did the woman ever really know what the artist meant? Had she ever entered into the artist's mind?

No. She had refused that possibility in the genteel way she managed most refusals, begging out because of lack of time and too many obligations. Before moving from Malibu onto the woman's land, V had urged the woman to spend time with her. The woman had always promised to visit V for longer than a few hours but she hadn't ever done it. Instinctively she knew about such border crossings. Physicists said that it was sometimes impossible to cross back and forth from one dimension into another. Once over the line, return was theoretical but not likely. One was altered and couldn't return except through progressive journeys, each one as perilous as the last.

Then the land where V was virtually squatting had been sold and she had had to move. Someone gave her a trailer and the woman invited her to put it on her own land and the artist had stayed with her. Briefly. For a year, or longer, the woman couldn't remember. It had been as if V had always been there and then as if she hadn't been there at all. If not for the trailer, the woman would have thought she had invented their connection altogether. In their months together, the woman learned very little about V and the way she lived. She suspected that V was living outside the trailer, using it only as her art studio, or to prepare her simple meals or to store her few things although her dishes, tools, artifacts were exquisitely arranged on shelves in a rough hewn outdoor shelter. When had that gone up? The woman couldn't remember. The woman never saw V enter or emerge from the trailer. In the morning, there she was drinking tea and again at night.

For all the time that V had lived with her, the woman had never spent an entire night outside in the manner that V might have been living all the time. They had visited in the woman's house, in the woman's manner, as if V's way of living did not exist. Until V arrived, the woman had always thought that her house, a good mile from the main road but still in the proximity of other houses, was exceedingly isolated even if she could see the lights of houses across the canyon. She had thought she lived in the bush and was puzzled that it wasn't a place where the artist felt comfortable living outside. The woman felt safe because of the proximity to others and endangered by the vastness, the extremity of it. But V said that living so close to the lights of houses and so much farther from the stars which they obscured, felt as if she were actually living inside everyone else. It was as if she were living in the mind of everyone whose light or house she could see, who had ever walked or driven up the road leaving permanent imprints of their noisy concerns.

On one occasion the woman had had a brief insight into V's mind. A man in a pickup truck had driven up the dirt road to the woman's cottage at high speed, music blaring and parked in front of her gate, so that it couldn't open. She came out another door, looked at the man slumped down in the driver's seat, eyes closed, grimacing, cap pushed back on his forehead, cigarette burning, flicking ashes on to the gravel next to the very dry brush, but otherwise immobile, "Dance me, dance me...."

The man hadn't noticed that she was there. He didn't seem capable of dancing. She didn't think he'd notice if the grass caught on fire and overcame him and his truck in a great conflagration. He was oblivious to her presence or his surroundings, as if the land was virgin and his.

Back in the house, she had called the police. The first cop car had arrived stealthily, but not slyly enough, for the man turned on the engine and spun the wheel hard right and drove over the entry walk into the meadow that slanted down from the house to the state park as if the steep, soft incline, the oak grove, the boulders, the soft soil wouldn't stop him. The woman had to exit the house boldly with her hands up and open to indicate her defenselessness and then point in the direction of the fugitive. To her surprise the cop didn't take off after the man but followed her inside and opted to remain there, both of them crouching down in the dark as the 911 operator had earlier instructed her. He had opened a window with his shotgun, she hadn't expected him to bring such a weapon in from the car and had said so. "870 Remington," he had answered — and she always prided herself in telling the story that she remembered that much, though he had said more about the gun that she could ever take in, as he was pushing open the screen so that it fell onto the azalea and camellia bushes, scattering the early red petals of spring. Then he had balanced the gun on his forearm, as if he could sight the man whose car was well below the hill. It was only when he saw how foolish he looked that he got up and out in time to greet his buddies who had just come up in a festival of spinning red. The woman was on her knees in the kitchen, not quite as low as the cop had advised, only low enough to satisfy the authorities while high enough to watch the hunt.

Outside, the man who didn't know what the woman knew, that the police were afraid, abandoned the truck that was quickly losing all speed, and ran, with the cops, now, five of them, after him. When he was cornered and shackled, the woman came out of the house and looked in his eyes. She didn't know if he saw her or not. He was crazed. Terror and drugs. The truck had been full of drugs. For a split second, she wanted to try them, each one of them, whatever they were in those neat plastic bags which zip locked so pleasantly. She wanted to know the mind that could drive up to someone's house, block her gate and put his head back on the headrest, and dream a dream of a fully intact world inside of him.

"You live here alone?" the first cop had asked.

She had found herself afraid of revealing that she did so she said nothing and as he did not find this unusual, he continued his casual conversation/interrogation with her.

"Hard to lock a house like this with so many glass doors. Wouldn't take much. A ball peen hammer gently knocks out one pane, in goes the hand, twist the latch, turn the door knob in. Don't you think?"

She hadn't wanted to say that she never locked her doors because she feared being broken into more than she feared being entered, and that she didn't want to pay more than she had to for the intrusion, so she was saving the cost of a pane of glass, the hard, transparent splinters, the crystalline evidence of will and malice.

V had certainly thought the road, though it was a dirt road, was far too close to the city and far too accessible, though all of the woman's friends and clients were urging her to pave it. V didn't want rural, she wanted wild.

Now the woman was sitting outside, even dozing for a few minutes at a time, with a young vulnerable in her lap to protect, and remembering that intrusion that might never have happened if she lived further away. What would V say now? Solitude had found V and called her to stones and boulders in Utah, some twenty miles from a town through a narrow canyon, and then across a mesa without any water, to a small flat area backing up to a line of rocky hills at the edge of a dry river strewn with more stones, boulders, small and great red presences, tumbling in the non-existent white water into pools of clay where lichen turned the patina of dry blood to pale, tentative green. V said she had been born from the stone people. She carved their hidden bodies, painted them blue, set them in circles, prayed among them. She said they spoke to her, long slow sentences taking days or weeks to form and she answered just as breathlessly and heaved in her sleep unafraid, ever, of the heaving of the earth.

After she had settled in, V called the woman from her base at the foot of the bluff, using a cellular phone, her single concession to her friends' alarm. V was a bit drunk on bravado, the woman had thought as V crowed, "No, no trailer yet. No need until next winter. You know, I got through this one."

"You didn't need to leave in winter."

"I didn't need to leave the land or you. I knew that. But I needed to leave. Don't worry. It's fun. This place, my lean-to, the car, solar panels for my computer. Yes, I put in a few posts and, planks in between to make shelves, and added some brass hooks and I've got a closet, a clothesline and a pantry. I seal everything in metal cans. Everyone is hungry out here."

But the woman hadn't gone out to visit V as soon as the snow melted as she had promised and the artist had hoped. She went several weeks later when she was giving a talk in the area and V wasn't there. The poles were there, two mugs attached. A lean-to. Jugs of water. V had begun to create a world she recognized, carving and smoothing the boulders, working with paint and chisel, so the eye followed a blue ripple of water across the head of the stone, or through a stony O carved to reveal a glimpse of the lace mantle of sky.

In the car with the girl, the woman returned to herself. Unusual justice, the artist leaving and the girl arriving. Not too many months in between. Just enough for the woman to know that the artist wasn't coming back and that she was lonely for someone else who might succeed in calling the woman out under the blue. Beyond the hills to the south, the sea was hidden from view, but its vapors, its foamy sea breath was creeping up the canyon at night through the narrow roads padding the green world with white cotton wadding until the clouds lowered altogether and the hills disappeared. She leaned back against the seat, adjusted her feet, dreamed.

On awakening to the woman stroking her hair, the girl said, "I'm not your pet." It was close to midnight.

"No," the woman acknowledged. "Alas, it would be so much simpler. And I'm not yours."

"You may be someday."

"I doubt it," the woman said. "I'm too old for such things."

"Not old enough," the girl said. "You're so cute," the girl said as if preparing to pet her, too.

"I doubt I'm cute," the woman said too quickly, a little miffed, uneasy about where the girl, now that she was awake, might take them, wondering how to maintain something she had been taught about boundaries. "Cute." The remark had a zipper effect. She was sitting straight and contained, like a house that had been shut in a panic when the rains had come, hard, driving and in a slant. It took only an instant to realize her pique had been an error as the girl withdrew and was cowering in a corner of the car. "Don't be afraid," the woman said tentatively reaching out her hand to stroke the girl and wondering what to do if the girl tried to bolt, would she be able to grab hold of her. If the gesture wasn't misguided, the thought was, for the woman quickly saw, but not quickly enough, that the girl understood the underlying intent of her gesture and also the thought, correctly, and took them both, as they had occurred simultaneously, as the woman's attempt to re-establish control. The girl's body moved very slightly but enough to indicate that she was withdrawing even further into herself, in another instant she would be entirely disappeared, dissolved into haze, mist, cloud, a smear of a white wolf dispersing soundlessly.

Thoughts, a silent argument and justification, swept through the woman's mind: "I'm trying to protect you. It's only for your own good. I'm afraid you'll run away. I'm afraid you'll run away and I'll be responsible. Carmela will kill me. I'm afraid you'll run away and I won't know what to do."

That was the truth of it. That and her fear that she (and then the girl) would sabotage this delicate balance that was being established between them, that she would continue to act in ways that were habitual or came out of training and that whatever gossamer peace was present between them would vanish. For a moment, she had intended to reassure the girl, or herself, that she was a professional and that implied a certain relationship — and hierarchy — between them. First of all it meant that she was in charge. That she was qualified. That nothing she was doing was personal. It was all a matter of good works.

She felt her own longing for the girl. For the girl to stay. For the girl to be safe here, to be happy. To find a perch for herself in the pepper tree. Guided by some genius she could not claim as her own, the woman put her open palm out toward the girl and said, "Smell. You can smell fear. I'm not afraid in the way you think. And I don't think I'm a pompous ass."

It was a gamble, this ordinary conversational tone. Was it a ruse or did she mean it? Could she settle into the tone? Could she find the truth of it inside her? Take it on, be faithful to it? Be an honest woman?

To her surprise, the girl took her hand after a few minutes and smelled the palm and the back of her hand and then her arm and then the soft spot just below the ear lobe. The scent had remained after all these hours.

"Sandalwood," the girl said. "Sandalwood." She did not seem to recognize the smell of her own piss or perhaps it had evaporated in the heat of the woman's momentary distress. Or perhaps she recognized it exactly as a wolf would recognize its own scent laid carefully at the boundaries of its territory.

The little bitch! The little bitch had marked her. The woman hadn't understood anything. The woman thought that she had been the one who was trying to entice the girl into her domain, when, in fact, the girl had marked her, had claimed her from the beginning, announcing to the entire world, or at the least the animal world which was the only one that concerned them now, "This one is mine."

"Do you want to come in my house now or do you want to see the trailer?"

The girl sat still as if she didn't understand anything the woman was saying and stared at the woman with great brown eyes that were both uncomprehending and fully comprehending. The woman relented to her instincts, to the flow of her nature, to the magnetism of the girl's presence and the night.

"There's the tree," she said, getting out of the car a bit stiffly, rubbing her lower back and then pointing to the pepper tree, whose branches were graceful as willows even though they emerged from a massive trunk that had split into five thick limbs rising at least fifteen feet in different directions so that the tree had span, created a shelter, sweet and pungent with tiny pink berries among the serrated leaves, a span that could, and later would, hide a small platform.

"But I would prefer to have you sleep in the house, tonight, tonight at least. Because I'm tired and don't want to worry about you all night. I've had enough."

It seemed the girl was thinking about this. What was worry? What was all night? What was enough? She made only the slightest gesture toward the woman but it was enough for the woman to understand. Not sure she was physically capable of what was required, she stepped closer to the car and leaned down slightly, but enough for the girl, still naked, to put her arms around the woman's neck and as the woman shifted to aright herself, the girl wrapped her skinny simian limbs about the woman's hips.

And still, the woman thought, as she carried the girl into the house and dressed her in a white nightgown with lace around the square neck and six pearl buttons down the front, the knife in the sheath still under the white fabric, and put her in her bed that the girl smelled like wolf, or spirit of wolf, and yet belonged in the white nightdress. In Little Red Riding Hood, the wolf, having eaten the grandmother, puts on the old lady's white night dress and night cap, and waits for the little girl to appear. They have definitely gotten it wrong, the woman thought. If anything, the grandmother had been waiting for the wolf in whatever form it deigned to appear. The wolf had not intended to impersonate any grandmother; it was the grandmother who wanted to be consumed by the wolf and so had arranged for Little Red Riding Hood to entice the wolf to her house so the old woman could give herself up in a sacrament of desire. Devouring Little Red had been an afterthought. Before she could comment on any of this, the girl was asleep again which was just as well as the woman had no training for such delicate conversations which need to take place under words. Better to attend to immediate concerns. Having taken on a daughter, she could only allow herself a quick shower, lathering her hair twice, before she, herself, settled down to sleep on the floor next to the bed.

Mist hovered closer and closer about the house. There was the sudden aroma of dark flowers, of Timber Wolf still lost in call and response, piercing cries of a night hawk and the soothing exchange of one owl and then another, baritone and alto, female and male, all of it sweet and peaceful. And then her own breathing and the breath of the girl. She didn't sleep at all as she kept the vigil, from time to time leaning over her small body to be certain she was alive, the girl's breath changing in the night, taking on the odor of mint and alcohol as if carrying the faint aroma of spirits.

D)aylight brought Carmela bounding up the driveway, buoyant, bouncy, carrying the girl's clothes and a few other items in brown paper bags up to the house before the girl awakened. It was a jocular transaction; they could have been at the supermarket. The woman stood still, her hands full, as Carmela drove off waving happily. Then she turned to convey the sweet burden to the trailer already feeling like a trespasser, knowing this was the last time she would enter without knocking at the door.

Coursing through the trailer with those shaky nervous gestures that come with sleeplessness, she quickly gathered up a bit of trash, swept out a few mouse droppings, made a mental note about Have-A-Heart traps, closed the empty drawers, opened them, arranged the girl's things neatly within them, tested the lights, changed a light bulb, scoured the sink and the toilet, changed the sheets on the single futon at one end of the trailer and opened the window that looked out across an olive tree to the face of the mountains opposite that bore a triangular scar, a sheer sheet of stone, three or four hundred feet long. The gash. It was an incision into the body of the mountain, the lips of the cut had been splayed open and the wound covered over with slate so that it was permanently agape.

She brought in a few dishes to add to what the artist had left, took the girl's clothes out of the drawers and laid them on the bed, better not assume anything, placed the other items once again in the brown paper bags and left them on the foldout table. There was water. The shower worked. The stove worked. Some propane remained. V had had a power line run from the woman's house. The electricity worked. The woman had an old bronze bell from China. It looked like a blowfish, leering. Through the slit of the mouth, one could see the rippled metal ball — someone had bothered to adorn it with lines of water — which made the fish sing. She put a wire through the arch at the top and hung it from a pole at the entrance to the trailer. The girl would have privacy and warning, if she wanted them.

As she was returning to her own house, she whistled for Timber who came immediately from his den under the far oleander bush, shaking off the poisonous white blossoms and dry leaves which had accumulated in his coat.

"You have to meet the girl," the woman was speaking, finally, as to an intelligent being instead of needlessly creating another far simpler language to communicate with him. In the past, he had indulged her. He had understood everything she had had to say even though she had simplified it. "I think she's going to stay here. Timber, we want her to stay. It may be up to you."

Old Timber, who understood both her words and the situation, slid in front of the woman and pushed open the front door with his nose, as he was often enjoined not to do, and went inside. Seeing the girl still asleep in the bed, he moved closer to prod her gently with his muzzle. She didn't awaken so much as put her hand down to his face and began rubbing the soft fur behind his ears. Then sure of him, she opened her eyes slowly.

"It's you," she said, stretching out the vowels into delight, catching the woman's eye but looking down immediately at the wolf, "Timber, it's you."

"Breakfast?"

The woman thought she was reading disdain for such a cheery question in the girl who turned back to the wolf and slid down to bury her face in his fur, letting him knock her gently to the ground, offering up her neck to his mouth, letting him lick her face, burying her own face in his neck. The two formed a circle, the woman was outside of it. Once again, she had misunderstood while Timber had not ever misunderstood her no matter how difficult she made communication with all her reductions and simplifications, but she had never understood him and had never bothered to learn his language or to determine if she was capable of it. The two creatures, girl and wolf, were together, where the woman had never been and might never be with all her supposed desire. She couldn't trust herself, couldn't be certain she meant the words she said or thought or felt. Couldn't trust them even before they were vocalized, couldn't trust them rising up inside of her like so much hope from a dark spring in the earth. There was a circle, the woman was outside of it; in order to step into the circle, she would have to cross one of those borders from which there is no return, she would have to take off all the garments of the self she had so carefully tailored, she would have to be more naked than the girl was, having now thrown off the silly white nightgown so she could roll skin to pelt with the old one who growled sometimes when she overwhelmed his bad hip but quickly nibbled or kneaded her in gestures of play and discovery. They were on the carpet, they were on the floor, they were out the door. The girl had understood the woman from the beginning and still, the woman thought — there she was thinking again — still, the girl had taken her on.

The woman waited to see if the girl was interested in eating. Then unsure of how to proceed, she went off into her study leaving the two, girl and wolf, together.

Sometime later, the girl entered the room after having followed Timber about the land, then to his place under the oleanders. Having learned something about his territory and her arena, she had come back to the house. Not knowing if the girl was naked or not, the woman had deliberately looked away. When she turned back, she saw the girl was, once again, a vision in the white night dress, but one that faded rapidly, as the girl in her dress, in clothes, was diminished, apprehensive, uncertain, despite her assumed posture of entitlement, hands on her hips.

"My things. I need to get my things."

"Carmela brought them."

"What about my car?"

"Where is it?"

"At Carmela's."

"I didn't see it yesterday."

"Stashed. I didn't want Carmela to see it and think I might run off in it and take the keys. Will you drive me to get it?"

"Are you staying then?"

Why did the woman ask that question? Did she want the girl to say, "Will you have me?" Did she want the girl to beg or reassure her? Or was the woman just asking the girl outright, "Will you have me?"

The way the woman was thinking, whatever the woman was thinking, clearly perplexed the girl and the woman couldn't stop even though she knew this was not the kind of question the girl liked to consider. From the girl's point of view, the woman's insistence could mean that she wanted her to make a formal declaration of acceptance, of appreciation, and through this acknowledgement invite the woman into a pack that now, clearly, included Timber as alpha wolf.

What did the woman want? Did she want the girl to grovel? Or did she want to be recognized as someone who would, who could do more or go further or understand more deeply than the other two women who hadn't been able to come toward the girl in the ways that mattered to her?

The woman had brought the girl home, yes. But she had not considered what this would mean on two counts. The fact of the house would alter what had occurred in the tree. And the scenario in the tree would certainly alter the ways and habits of the house. At the tree, the woman had imagined, allowed everything — girl, wolf, spirit, appearance and disappearance, the original manifestations of creation, coming and going.

But in a house, things should be settled, shouldn't they? House was, after all, one of the distinctions between here and there, between woman and animal, between real and dream. One built a house and settled down. Was this what she was thinking? She wasn't wanting to be thinking. She had instincts too. Not animal instincts, necessarily but imposed reflexes that had become like instincts. Instincts for order and solidity. Instincts about the way things were done in her domain. Rules. Laws. Agreements. Contracts. Property. Territory. Boundaries. All of it. If you lived in a house you were as good as nailed to the cross beams. House did that.

The girl raised her dark eyes and stared at the woman without blinking, with the implacable gaze of a cow, let's say, or the large undaunted eyes of a large ape, the certain and fearless gaze of any large mammal confronting a smaller, skittering, nervous creature who wasn't at home in the world. Whatever the woman wanted, she was not going to get.

"Will you drive me to get the car?"

It was the answer but it was said in a little girl's voice, a girl hardly old enough to drive, a girl not quite tall enough to reach the gas pedals or see over the steering wheel. They were going to hell fast and the woman didn't know how to shift gears. The last one to be in charge of this situation was the woman and she didn't know how to get herself out of the tight spot she had designed.

"I will." A good start. "Can we eat first?" Big mistake.

"Depends...." The girl didn't know if the woman had any flexibility at all.

"On what?" She probably had no flexibility.

"We'll see...." The girl was playing for time.

It wasn't such a conversation exactly. There were long pauses between the woman's responses and the girl's words. Spaces so long the woman would forget what she had said while drifting into the girl's sense of time, vast.

"What do you call breakfast?" Suddenly anything the woman might consider breakfast, even if she never had anything but coffee until late afternoon, would not be considered breakfast by the girl. "Coffee, birdseed, anything you want."

"I usually have a hot chocolate drink. That's why I need my things. The chocolate comes from South America; I need my pot and bowls. They're in my car."

"I could improvise something that might come close."

"No, I don't think so," the girl did not appreciate the thought of improvisation. "I can wait."

"Cocoa... Or I can make toast. You should eat ...." What difference did it make, really, if they ate now, or later, her food or the girl's? Still she backtracked, "Or eggs. What about eggs? I can manage an appropriate bowl. When you finish the cocoa, you'll see white flowers at the bottom. I can make you rice and beans. Black beans. Red beans. I have a bean pot. I got it in San Blas. Of course, it will take a while.

"Are you game?" When the woman reflected on herself, she felt the hysteria within herself and tried to slow down her words, use fewer of them.

'What kind of rice?'

"Basmati or jasmine, your choice." "Your choice" had been unnecessary.

"Let me see."

"Shall I show them to you or tell you where they are so you can find them yourself?" That's what she would have said a few moments ago. Finally, she acquiesced. "Okay."

The girl slid down from the bed to which she had returned, the woman following her, and though it seemed that she stood upright, it also seemed to the woman that she was on all fours and the woman, once again, couldn't distinguish the girl from the various animal shapes she assumed. Timber went into the next room which was half kitchen and half living room and lay down in his place alongside the chaise which marked the division in the room and guarded the entry to the patio, the woman's study, and the bathroom beyond, all at the same time. From the center of the universe, sentinel before all entrances, he watched the girl scuttle past him toward the couch at the back end of the room and squeeze herself into the very narrow space on the floor between the couch and the wall.

Except that the girl had almost disappeared alongside the couch, it was perfectly ordinary, exactly perfect, exactly what the woman had hoped for: woman, girl, wolf, morning, sunlight, breakfast. The woman knew that the wolf was watching the girl but not because he was going to pounce on her. The wolf had discerned that the girl was one of his own and he had made a decision: He was going to care for the girl. Already there was an aroma in the room; it was the musk of intimacy between them. It wasn't that they liked the scent and so it drew them to each other; it was that they were drawn to each other and this attraction had a scent, left a mark on the territory of their connection. She could see it, whatever it was, that was between them, an eddy in an invisible field that flowed out of them and washed about them. And out of this, the delight of recognition, which, again, was not recognition, but the annulment of difference. A common world made evident through the faintest fragrance, a smear of self on the wind that travels between here and there. It was intoxicating and then it vanished. The girl was cowering in the corner and Timber lay with his back to her, his head on his paws, his eyes closed. It was the woman's move.

"There's your friend's flute," the girl said, her eyes, momentarily filled with tears. The wooden flute that was scratched and so carelessly assembled that the mouthpiece did not accord with the finger holes had been thrown into a basket of, admit it, noisemakers. "Is it mine, now?" the girl asked tremulously.

The tone of the flute, as the girl played it, was light and quavering as a hummingbird, as cicadas. It became a quena, the forbidden flute, therefore endangered. The girl receded as if into the wall itself.

Carmela hadn't done it differently, the woman admitted to herself as she set a kettle to boil, held up two packages of rice, brought them to the girl who didn't blink. The woman retreated, washed the Basmati rice after considering, if hopelessly, which was most appropriate for breakfast, put on the rice cooker, examined her dishes until she found the brown clay bowl with the white petals, from the market at San Blas, and sat down facing the girl who was visibly shivering. Who was trembling.

Even when the woman retrieved a teapot she hadn't used for years from an open shelf where it had been mere decoration, washed it, ladled cocoa powder into the porcelain holder and set it waiting, everything with the girl was no go. The girl was not comforted by the woman's proximity. She was receding even further into the tiny space, perching atop the pile of old newspapers with her hands at her sides as if ready to spring. Quaking. What had the woman done?

Timber moved around to the front of the chaise to observe the girl who had been blocked from his view. The woman wished that the wolf could speak plain English. She looked for thoughts in her mind that she could attribute to the wolf and couldn't find any.

What would she do if the girl had been a small animal? Timber had shivered when she had first brought him home, a small bundle of fear that had scampered away from her to the darkest and most inaccessible places, under the beds, behind doors, into closets, into the cabinet under the sink in a scatter of scouring powder, cans, sponges and Brillo pads. Accordingly, she had become very quiet and very small, down on her own hands and knees, large towel in hand, she had quietly pursued the terrified creature, gathering him up into a soft cloth and bundling him against her, opening both blouse and towel and placing him against her body. She had breathed to him as she imagined a wolf mother might breathe while the pup nestled against mammary glands and heartbeat. It was not about language, fast or slow, complex or simple, not about any language the woman knew. It was about another way of knowing, an intelligence the woman had only managed once or twice.

She took the blanket from the back of the couch, opened it, pressed it against her chest, and moved, blanket open toward the girl, humming the cradle song, reaching finally around the girl and letting the blanket fall over the girl's slim shoulders. The girl didn't move and so the woman pressed on gathering the girl to her, urging her out of the corner, down onto the floor, unzipping her shirt and letting the girl's face fall alongside her neck and collar bone, willing her pulse to be strong against the girl's cheek, willing her heartbeat strong against the girl's chest, until the trembling subsided and all the time praying that she wouldn't speak, that she wouldn't be tempted to say anything that would remind the girl that the woman was definitively and irreversibly a (foolish) human being.

When the convulsive fear subsided, the woman brought the food. A pot of chocolate. Rice in the painted clay bowl. Two cups. Plates. No beans. They would be ready in a few hours. A tangerine, peeled and separated. Crackers. A plate with several white and yellow cheeses. She had no idea what the girl might eat. Corn was all she could think of and she had none in the house. She put everything on the nearby table and then thought better of it. She put it all on the floor, leaned back against the blue couch said a silent prayer and very, very slowly began eating.

The girl was elsewhere. Her eyes were closed. She was humming something. The woman smelled her breath on her cheek like a breeze. The woman ate hoping the girl would eat too. Then overcome with drowsiness, the woman stretched out, put her head on an Indian mirrored pillow from the couch, the small, reflecting circles embroidered in place with blue and gold threads in the pattern of stars, and curled up as if sleeping in that place was the most natural, the most irresistible thing in the world.

And slept. She didn't know how long she had let her attention wander, she couldn't say it was sleep, even to herself in her own mind. Awakening with her eyes closed still, she surveyed the room, listening. The refrigerator, Timber's deep breathing close to her and something else, something wakeful. She opened her eyes. The girl was staring at her as if she was a strange creature herself, something never seen before. The girl was hunkered down by the woman's head. Her hand was on Timber's head which was wedged next to the woman. The girl's bowl was next to the woman, half empty. The girl's face was just a few inches from her own face and her eyes were deep with benevolent curiosity. She had a wedge of tangerine in her hand with a small bite, as of a mouse, taken out of it. She passed it over the woman's lips, making her smile, the way a mother might entice a smile out of an infant. The girl smiled too then. And made another pass with the tangerine. The woman licked her lips and smiled again. With the lightest of touches, the girl pressed the tangerine against the woman's lips insisting she nibble on it. Then she took what remained and put it in her own mouth savoring the juices. And finally, with the feather her fingers had become, the girl traced all the lines on the woman's face, crow's feet spreading out from her eyes, the beginning of gullies down from her nose, the little puckers on her chin, the lines across her forehead, the slash between her eyebrows that had been there since childhood.

Upon this line, the proof of the woman's constant perplexity, her desire to see deeper, the squint into understanding, the girl lavished such tenderness that the woman found tears rolling down her cheeks from eyes that had mysteriously filled. This didn't daunt the girl. She took a tear onto her forefinger and placed it in her mouth. And then another. Until, it seemed as if she had drunk all the woman's tears.

It wasn't a voice really, it was a warble, the woman thought, or a coo, the soft hushing of something small, feathered and nested which seemed to be saying, "You're nice. Very nice." She hoped she was right, had understood correctly these first words spoken in what it seemed was the girl's own language.

"Let's get the car."
"Now?"
"Now."
"Good. Put Timber in the back seat."
"It's a deal."

And that is how it happened. That is what it took for the woman to find herself the next day seated once again on the floor with her back against the couch with the girl, who had not yet slept in the trailer but on the floor beside the woman's bed, exactly where the woman had slept the night before. So when the woman awoke, because she had not slept the previous night and also because she had felt safe, safe that the girl would be there in the morning, went into the living room and took up her place on the floor leaning against the couch, this small animal, a wary bobcat, or even more tremulous rabbit, came out of the cave she had made between the couch and the wall, and sniffed the woman's square hands, verifying, "Sandalwood," before she settled down. That was all it took for her to put her head in the woman's lap, extending one hand to Timber Wolf while her other hand held tightly to the woman's hand, who, with her other hand was stroking the girl's hair.

"What shall I call you?" Carmela had had a name for her but it was important to begin again.

"Azul," the girl said.

"Why that's the name I would have chosen myself. I would have called you Blue."

The girl wrinkled up her nose to indicate that the woman hadn't gotten it right. "I've had it a long time," said the girl, "longer than you can imagine. Since before the time I was born."

"What name would you like to give me?" the woman asked because she was afraid to hear what Azul would say. Azul turned her head so that they were looking in each other's eyes.

"Owl Woman is your name."

Owl Woman. Better than she had dared to hope.

"Doña Tia Tecolote. That's your name, Owl Woman."

Many gifts came with the name, respect accompanied Doña, the kind of respect that wasn't familiar to the woman but was extended to honored members of the family, to the matriarchs and elders in the girl's culture. And love came with Tia, the kind of love also that wasn't familiar to the woman, but that she knew had existed among family members in the old country. Then the acknowledgment of vision, wisdom, a piercing and unrelenting gaze, and the soft white down beneath a miraculous bed of speckled feathers that Owl denoted. Tecolote. She hadn't expected the girl to bring her joy.

There they were: It was the beginning of the world. The girl was naming the animals over which she would have dominion and the woman was, herself, growing alert, wrapping talons around a perch, seeing 360 degrees into the landscape of the girl's mind, wanting the small warm mouse, wanting soaring, perspective and distance. Indeed, closing her eyes, she found that she had wings, that she could soar, that she could leap from this height and land without a rustle of a leaf on that branch there, and in between only speed, focus and flight.

"I want a story, I want you to tell me a story, Owl Woman," the girl said. "One that makes you happy and sad at the same time."

"Like all good stories," the woman said as she began:

"Once upon a time, in the great green woods, there lived a young girl whose name was Azul."

"Once upon a time, in the great woods..." Azul repeated. "It has been a long time, Owl Woman, since I've been in the great woods, I can hardly remember how it was."

"When were you in the woods, Azul?"

"Before."

"Before what?"

"Before everything, Owl Woman. When I was happy."

"And when..."

"And when....?" The silence that followed the girl's imitation of the woman's questioning was tense rather than profound. When the girl was in the tree, it had been obvious who was up and who was down.

The woman heard the girl's silent, pointed rebuke in her own mind: "Professional curiosity, Owl Woman? Is this an intake interview? Are you looking for a diagnosis? Or did you learn this line of questioning in Interrogation 101?" Azul didn't let her continue.

They had reached another impasse. Admit it. It had pleased the woman to think that she could, once again, be a few jumps ahead of the girl. For the girl's sake, of course. In order to take care of the girl. In order to help her. Why help her? Because she was clearly suffering. Why did the woman think so? Because .... Because the girl had been in a tree. Because the girl had been trembling. It was obvious, wasn't it. Obvious? Did Azul think she was suffering? It hadn't occurred to the woman to consult the girl on this matter. There were symptoms. Complexes. And there was Carmela's original assessment of the situation as if the woman had ever trusted Carmela on any matters of consequence.

Carmela had said the girl was in trouble and Owl Woman had acted accordingly. And now the girl had said, or implied, that she wasn't happy but had been at one time. Wasn't that sufficient cause? The girl had been happy at one time, ergo she wasn't happy now. That was an unhappy situation that the woman was divinely inspired to fix. Right? The woman could barely keep herself from laughing out loud at herself. Happy! Did she know anyone who was happy? Was happiness any more than a late twentieth century invention? Should one strive for it? Was it a serious path?

As was becoming familiar, the woman found herself lost once more in musing about a new development which threw the entire (new) relationship into disarray if not all the relationships Owl Woman had had with anyone else. Things she had taken for granted. Her own judgment, for example....

"When was I happy? It depends," Azul was saying, "if you look at things from the outside in or the inside out."

"How do you look at things, Azul?"

"From the inside out, of course. From anyone's insides out. It's easier to see out than to see in. I use only natural light. You come in with a searchlight thinking you will see everything. But really all you see is your own flare bouncing about."

"What do you want, Azul?" The woman was exasperated which meant that she was bumping up against things she once thought she understood.

"Don't dis me. Just because you got me out of a tree, doesn't me you have the right to dis me."

"I wouldn't...."

"You just did inside your mind. Are you going to tell me a story to tell me a story or are you going to tell me a story for what you people call therapeutic purposes? Are you trying to unravel or tie up my mind? When I get inside your mind, I don't like the look of me when I'm looking out of you at myself."

"What do you see, Azul?"

"Back off, lady."

The movement was infinitesimally small. Not a motion really, only the fleeting thought of a move, a mammalian instinct toward readiness, the body alerted, remembering claw, fang, jaw, pounce. On the woman's part, her reflex was equally precise. She was ready too. The woman had shifted her glance to the girl's hand and the knife in the sheath. Knowing where the danger lay, preparing herself for any quick assault, instinctively scheming to disarm rather than harm the girl, these preparations made them equals.

"You're fast, Owl Woman." Azul was laughing. "I keep being afraid that I'm going to have to take care of you exactly when I'd rather pummel you to death. This takes a weight off my shoulder. It looks like we can both take care of ourselves.

"Now tell me a true story, my dear, dear Tecolote."

"You mean about myself?"

"No, that would never be true. Make up a story. Make up a true story. About the girl in the woods. The one you call Azul. About her."

It was just the beginning, but it was already the way life was between them. The girl postulated an entire universe by her mere existence. She did not solicit the woman's assistance in creating this world, but she might ultimately depend, the woman was surmising, on the woman's inclination and ability to enter that world. On the woman's ... ? ... on the woman's delight! Nothing the woman had experienced in her personal or professional life had prepared her for such a seduction.

This is the way it had started. The girl had been brought to her because she was ... suffering... because... she was ... in trouble. Because.... The woman had always refused to use the professional language which, pretending to diagnose, pinned a person to pathology and left them dangling. So she wouldn't, even in what had been the secrecy of her own mind before Azul's appearance, use that terminology, not even to the extent of ... no... she wouldn't, didn't, let the words enter her consciousness even to review which of those she refused. Carmela had not known what to do with a girl in a tree, with a girl who had no home, no friends, it seemed, no kin, no telephone, no visible means of support, who was often in fear and trembling, whimpering sometimes, or howling, who sometimes ate and sometimes didn't, who sometimes spoke and sometimes didn't, who washed or didn't, slept or didn't, wore a knife, saw what others saw or didn't, saw other things they didn't see, was reliably neither here nor there. Bless Carmela for trying. A friend in common had told Carmela the girl wanted to rent a room for a short time, while she was looking for work or returning home, and though Carmela already had a roommate, she had agreed, to be agreeable. Bless Carmela.

Now the girl was here and it was nothing like what the woman had expected. It was not a professional situation. Never had been and never... she faltered... but couldn't deny her own convictions, ... never ... should have been.

What, the woman thought, if the way that Azul was living was not proof that she was shattered, was not a symptom of being out of her mind, was not a sign that she was crazy or crazed by the circumstances of her life? What if she was not acting this way in response to the enormity of her pain? What if she was in great pain and still Azul had not been "acting out?" What if Azul's behavior was not aberrant? What if ... healing... was not modulating or diminishing or removing these behaviors by relieving or reliving what she had suffered in the past?

Yes, the girl had suffered. So what. No, that wasn't the direction either. Yes, the girl had suffered. Yes, her past had been dreadful. Yes, the girl was howling and trembling. Like Timber had, or did, in the face of ... what? ... in the face of circumstances that impinged upon his spirit, that limited or endangered wolf in the world. That's what made him howl with grief. Otherwise the howl was an extreme aria of joy, a paean to beauty, an extended exultant vowel climbing solo or in concert heavenward.

In that moment, she looked out the window and saw two woodpeckers climbing in tandem, heads bobbing, up the telephone pole and now triumphant at the top, making their ways across the horizontal pole in opposite directions to the two ends, pausing, and then, in one motion, flying up together, landing and perching like two stars on the pointed crown of the adjacent deodar cedar, what the Hindus called the Timber of the Gods.

Hoping that the girl would no longer howl or would not live in trees might not be a sensible goal of healing. Maybe healing lay elsewhere. Maybe the girl's soul was seeking the right perch, a nightingale singing her heart out, or a wild creature unimpeded by civilization, howling her heart out, a white wolf at the peak of a snow mountain whose far vision still encountered deep blue shadows cast on pristine white. Maybe healing need not and would not occur in the girl but between the girl and the woman by compelling, calling forth, re-enforcing, re-establishing a little world they could both inhabit. Safely. Happily.

Azul. The world around the girl was turning blue and everything in it altering to harmonize with the color so that sound, activity, experience were modulated melodiously. Blue was not merely a gel through which one saw the same world. Blue shaped the world. Blue was another world entirely with its own laws and manifestations. Blue changed everything, the relationships and the essence of what it fell upon.

The girl lived in Blue. She was who she was because she had fallen into and decided to live in and take on the qualities of Blue. Accordingly, she had taken its name as an emblem or a sign but also knowing the intrinsic relationship between self and name, she became her name much as her name became her.

Finally, the woman saw that the girl was gifted with the means of knowing who might join her in Blue and who were by their own nature barred from ever entering. The woman wanted to enter. She wanted to live in Blue. At least some of the time. She was waffling. She wanted to claim it also as her territory too. Her God-given territory too. No, no, not folie á deux, but a real and viable world, albeit profoundly and continuously assaulted.

OK, the woman convinced herself. This was the direction. But what, the inner voices began again with their familiar segue: What if the girl didn't get better? What if her symptoms didn't disappear?

The hell with symptoms, the woman said. None of this matters. What matters is only that the girl feels entitled to live in Blue and has a companion there. She didn't know how long she would remember or understand this insight, but for the moment she rested in its glow.

"Blue," she said, "Azul," letting the uuuu of Blue become the uuuu of Azul, using the vowel itself to carry her across and hearing, even as she was carried by the reverberation of it, that it was a howl, a howl that didn't belong to wolf alone, a howl that was intrinsic to Blue. And even as she said the word, as she uttered it, uttered the UUUU she could feel that something was shifting in her, that she was being altered by the proximity of the ululation, by having taken in the sounds — she was lost in them — the uu uuu uuu uu uu UUU UUU UUUUU UUU uu uu uu uu uuuu entering into her body like a Host.

"You were going to tell me a story, remember?"

"Once upon a time, in the great woods, there lived a young girl whose name was Azul. She was a silent girl who moved without sound, more like a wind can slip between one leaf and another without sign of disturbance."

It was easy once she was in it to get lost in the story. There had probably once been a path and purpose, but it was gone within the first sentence. The words opened up before her as if she were indeed in the jungle, dropped off in the middle of a green tangle of great trees and vines. She didn't know where she was and she had to go forward. Desire was pulling her the way fear, ambition or good works had pulled her in the past. She was telling a love story. Yes, that was it. She was telling the girl how much she loved her in a way that was permissible.

"A strange and silent girl who moved through the woods as if she had been born to trees. The girl had learned the many languages of beast and birds, had learned howls, growls, barks, bugles, snarls, trills, whistles, cheeps, chirps, screeches, squawks, warbles, caws, coos and hoots." The woman found herself laughing as she searched for more sounds and imagined making them.

"Which languages did she speak?"

"She spoke jay and dove, she spoke finch, owl and crow, she spoke wolf, coyote, deer, rabbit and mouse. But there was one language she didn't speak and that was the language of lizard. Lizard was so silent, even more silent than the girl, that Azul had never been able to catch a word."

"That's not his name," Azul said, "Iguana, that's his name. The silent one. Don Iguana Silencio. You'll have to know him better, Owl Woman, if you want to tell his story. Let me sleep, Owl Woman, while you go about your business. I'm tired and I'm crowded and I'm not used to living around people and I'm not certain I like it very much."

There were things the woman thought she'd never get used to that became familiar. The sight of an old blue convertible with a garland of dried blue straw flowers draped across the windshield parked in front of her door each day, exactly positioned — it could not be easy to arrange — so that the headlights shone directly into her house as if the girl were searching through every corner of her life. Flute music from the top of the pepper tree almost any hour but the ones that the woman had once deemed appropriate. Moonrise or moonset music. Midnight music. Music of the Andes and the Sierra Nevada. The sight of bare brown feet, appearing, disappearing. Tiny morsels of food, a peach with one (tiny) bite taken from it, half of a wedge of apple, four blueberries, balls of mango and papaya, a single cracker, the tiniest silver fish, narrower than a forefinger which had been delicately fried, a thimble full of rice scooped into a miniature zucchini, three tangerine crescents left here and there on tables, arm rests, on the floor by the chaise. Or the opposite, large bowls of highly seasoned foods, Mexican, Brazilian, Central American, Thai, Chinese, Japanese made with elaborate sauces, chilies, molé, ginger, lemon grass, spices she had never encountered, left on her table. A door opening so quietly one thought one was imagining the gap between jamb and door edge and a hand darting in to set a dish of green beans with tomatoes, garlic and peppers, a corn casserole, a bowl of *sopa de ajo* on the floor. The girl's refusal to use the woman's dishes or to take back her own until the woman belatedly realized that the girl had made the dishes herself, that it was her vocation — that Carmela had known nothing of this — and that each bowl was as much a gift as the food. And soon, though no word was spoken, the woman found it necessary to add a set of shelves to her office, one of the four small rooms in her house, where she displayed these delicate artifacts.

Sometimes finding tiny gifts, no, minute offerings of stained glass, some the size of silver dollars, miniature rose windows, mandalas of angels or corn maidens, the Virgin with piranhas nursing at her breasts or bats with cobalt blue butterfly wings. Sometimes equally tiny drawings on translucent papers, or paintings on glass, a medicine wheel with four shamans dreaming peyote, a miniature gouache of open-mouthed masks of deer with vultures for tongues and jaguars for eyes, tiny silver dolphins leaping and copulating on fine gold chains, charcoal drawings of fishhooks in the eyes of whales, a diminutive oil painting of Quetzalcoatl, the winged serpent rising out of the navel of the girl's own body, then a self-portrait of the girl herself, emerging out of a mask of Frida Kahlo, crucified and ecstatic on a world tree encircled with lianas and serpents. Unimaginable how tiny these pieces, how subtle and complex they were, that any human could have made them. She cherished them for as long as she had them for they were, like gifts of flowers, temporary. They appeared and disappeared according to their own seasons which only the girl knew. Sometimes they reappeared in the girl's trailer hanging from chains or wires or affixed to the windows so the woman was always startled on sunny days by the dark rainbows, claret, burgundy, vermilion, turquoise, emerald, topaz, amber, ruby, malachite, and amethyst that flooded the room. Only after a long time did the woman also come to know that these were pieces of a puzzle, the interior of the girl's mind and that someday the girl would lay them all out and assemble them into a single window and the woman and girl would look through the mosaic at the light of another world.

But until then, different scenarios. Hours spent sometimes trying to entice the girl to eat something, anything. Having to swallow numerous vitamin pills to prove they weren't poisonous. The sight of a field mouse or a fruit rat in the girl's lap; the way she caught them in the safe traps and gentled them afterwards with nibbles of crackers and peanut butter and let them go; but they never ran far from her. A small body burrowed into a mound of grass, a snippet of cloth or sighting of toe peeking out of scrub oak. The girl's intractable nature. Her unwillingness to be inside when anyone else would choose to be inside or her refusal to be outside when everyone was out.

"Why do you sleep outside? Your body is being devoured by mosquitoes and chiggers." There were bites in various stages of eruption and healing up and down Azul's arms and legs. Azul hadn't noticed them particularly as if she willingly let anything feed from her body.

Ribbons tied to trees marking the girls passage across the hills or indicating a particular prayer, blue for the reappearance of wolves, brown for bears, yellow for the yellow eyes of the cougars, green for the trees, red for the Chumash peoples, scarlet for her own peoples though who they were, she wouldn't say. An apparition in white, the girl floating across the land in the white nightdress the woman had given her that first night, which was almost all she wore, using an antique porcelain basin to wash off the smears of different colored clays she gathered each day and hanging the dress in the apricot tree outside her trailer before she went to bed and then putting it on in the morning after mending its tears and embroidering over its stubborn stains so it was covered with the same tiny roses, robins, salamanders, spiders that adorned her bowls and plates and stained glass but these rendered in rose, periwinkle, silver, green and gold threads.

And finally the woman's need to distinguish in every moment the girl's pain calling out to be noticed, eased or attended, or to be ignored, from the girl's invitation to create camaraderie.

The woman wasn't skilled at this and more often erred in the direction of pain to be relieved, disintegration to be stopped, or illness to be rooted out than she succeeded in recognizing that the girl was calling her, calling her forth, for the woman's own sake. Because now that Blue was penetrating all things, it didn't mean that the world into which the woman had been born, and where she was still living most of the time when she wasn't with Azul, no longer existed. It existed, one could say, more emphatically than it ever had before and the woman had no skills in living in two worlds at once.

Several months after they began to live on the land together, the girl, who had cooked for the woman, was refusing to eat the food herself, though she always made the woman eat what the woman had cooked before Azul tasted it. The girl had been refusing to eat for days. Further, Azul was refusing to enter the house or her trailer, insisting that she was going to spend yet another cold, rainy night outside under the tree wearing, once again, only the white night dress. Desperate, the woman devised guerrilla tactics that violated the unspoken agreements between her and the girl. She enlisted Timber's assistance.

Never in the moment, but after some useless struggle or conflagration that left the woman disappointed in herself and the girl embittered, did Owl Woman remember that the hierarchy of girl and woman had disappeared, had become obsolete in the first moments she had encountered the girl in the tree. Owl Woman had been prepared for this by her years with Timber. It was very difficult, if not impossible, to train a wolf. He would accommodate himself to her demands only if they suited him, only if they displayed an intelligence that was greater than his in the moment. He was very discerning about what served and didn't serve his nature and his life. The woman was discovering over these weeks that it was equally impossible to shape Azul to her own ways of thinking, to — and now she certainly sounded like Carmela and Dusty — what anyone would deem civilized. The woman was also learning how very difficult it was for her to change her own behavior; how very difficult it is to teach an old dog new tricks. She finally conceded that she could do nothing to control the girl or the situation, so her efforts were better spent trying to find a way that she and the girl could meet. But, in order for them to really meet, the woman had to get down from her high horse. How well she had come to understand that phrase.

The woman, who was circling around the pepper tree as close to the girl as she was permitted, pacing, determined — also wet, cold, uncomfortable — called Timber outside to her and he, hearing in her voice, both worry and acquiescence, came, without reluctance, though he had been warm and dry in the house. He yielded to her concern as if he understood that only his intent would prevail with the girl. This was the crucial moment, but the woman couldn't have put words to it, and why should she, if it was the wolf who was bringing her to the crossroads she had so inadequately imagined.

It had started off so humbly. She wanted the girl in the house. She wanted her dry. She wanted her to eat. Yes, she could hear those words inside her head, "I want," "the girl should," "it will be best if she..." Will. Her will. It would never do. The woman was presuming what the girl repeatedly indicated was not presumable, that the woman had superior knowledge, understanding and perspective. It was also presumed that the girl did not have these because she was in pain. Pain and difficulties erased wisdom and self-knowledge. That was an underlying, unspoken, presumption. And so it wasn't a matter of the girl's location after all, wasn't a matter of the girl being here or there, but was, as it was turning out, a matter of the woman's location in relationship to her species and its presumptions.

Well then, without another thought because what she called thinking would not do now that she was trying to be articulate and conscious in the world that Azul and Timber agreed upon, the woman dropped down to her hands and knees on the wet earth. As a strategy it was absurd, but as a ritual act, a gesture of deference, it had merit. Timber approached her directly and when she greeted him nose to nose, yielding to him, even with a slight movement of her neck offering herself, her better judgment, up to him not in defeat but with trust, he turned and, yes, it was unmistakable, circled with his great head, shook himself to demonstrate that he was uncomfortable in the rain, and so invited both girl and woman to follow his lead.

In such a manner, what the woman would later call her initiation had begun. The woman crawled as if she were also four-legged, across the muddy ground. It was essential to do this without imagining that she was stooping to something beneath her; she had to find dignity in this position. Before she wiped her palms, knees and toes on the mat and entered the house, she examined the earth on her hands. This is not a stain, she told herself. It may stain the carpet but it is not a stain on my hands. Only when she was crossing the threshold did she stop to see if the girl was behind them. She was. But not on all fours like the woman. She was quite erect, striding into the house a bit amused, a bit perplexed. As if the woman was daft and she had been coming in on her own all along. As if she had only been waiting for Timber to indicate the way.

The first test the woman had to pass came as soon as she was in the house. The manner of rising up onto her feet was essential; the woman had to become erect again without losing anything, neither the girl nor herself, nor dignity.

In this negotiation, the wolf could not help her, nor, of course, would the girl, except with peals of laughter. Puzzling this dilemma, she didn't notice that the girl had slid down to the ground, not in camaraderie with the woman but in order to romp with Timber. There they were the two of them, girl and wolf, enfolded one into the other, nuzzling each other, unaware of her anguish and confusion, which was comforting, and also indifferent to her, which was disturbing. How was she to reach across the abyss between herself and them, the abyss that had swallowed all of human history in one ravenous bite?

The moment was critical. She stretched up as Timber stretched horizontally and then attentive to what animal grace she thought she might have, she took the girl's supper that she had originally placed on the table, three bowls — the girl's bowls — containing rice, fried bananas and ceviche the girl had prepared the night before and slid them onto the floor. The girl pretended not to understand. She slunk off into her corner between the couch and the wall. The woman continued, putting out a plastic bowl of food for Timber. The girl looked on with disdain. The woman took the two plates from the shelf she had laid out for herself and Azul and placed them on the floor next to Timber. No silverware. And then slid onto the floor again next to them.

"I'll get water," the girl said and brought back a water bowl — the woman hadn't seen this one — with Timber's face painted on the bottom of it, his yellow eyes staring, and two glasses, setting the water bowl before

Timber first, as the woman saw, not because of his wolfish thirst, nor even as a sign of respect for an elder, but because she loved him.

And then she drew the woman to her whispering, "Come here, my little one," in exactly the manner the woman had used with her so many times, and stroked her hair the way she always stroked Timber, the lightness of her touch, the tenderness of it.

They ate the bananas silently. Then, perhaps, it was a miraculous moment of understanding, the woman and the girl exchanged glances, and, simultaneously, both rose to their feet and took their bowls to the table again. The girl got silverware, but without any indication of disdain. The woman placed the table napkins without triumph. They sat down to what remained of the meal with utter casualness and the woman managed not to say anything when the girl slipped away to the bathroom and returned in the khaki shorts, knife sheath attached to its belt, and a dry tank top and jacket that she had stashed away there. She offered the woman a shawl. Their relationship was precisely negotiated without a word being said.

There was nothing in her professional literature that could inform the woman about the rhythms that the two of them entered. As they didn't speak much in any depth or particularity, it was as easy for the woman to associate the peaks and dips in their relationship with sunspots as anything else. The girl didn't speak about herself and the woman believed it would be inappropriate for her to reveal anything private about herself except what was revealed in the intimacy of their daily life, which was shared or not shared, depending upon the mood or inclination of the girl.

The woman pursued her work. Clients came and went. The girl, alerted to the cars, was always out of sight. The woman was watchful, observing herself carefully to see if and when these new circumstances were influencing her work with others. She was wise enough to know they would have to have some impact. She was perhaps more vigilant with her clients than she had been before. After all, Azul was Azul and the others needed to be met equally for who they were and what they needed. It seemed to the woman that her clients were making progress, were — happier. That word again. They seemed to like being in her house and commented more than they had in the past about appreciating meeting in a home setting rather than an office. Or maybe they liked the fruit, canapés, little tidbits, small plates of dried berries and nuts that the girl left for what she called the woman's guests.

For days at a time, Azul would be occupied, or preoccupied, the woman wasn't certain which, and stayed in her trailer, painting, or reading, or writing, or ... sleeping. She slept a lot, inside and outside, but without any discernible pattern.

One day, quite spontaneously, the girl began to speak about her past. "I once had a dog," the girl said. "But he got killed. A man was hunting in the woods. He was hunting me. He got Perito."

The story of the dog emerging in fragments and stutters never became coherent. It began and trailed off. Sometimes the dog was taken to the pound; sometimes, its name was Perita and she had been run over by a car and left to die; sometimes he, Perito, was run over by a car driven by a stranger, sometimes by someone Azul knew. Once he had been killed accidentally by Azul's father as he was backing out of the garage; sometimes the creature was run over deliberately by Azul's *abuelo*, or her *tio*, Eduardo, or by a neighbor, by someone who had known that the dog would stand his ground against any car and meanly proceeded to challenge it, exerting his will. Sometimes the dog had run out into the street and threw himself under the wheels of a car speeding by.

The woman was fascinated by the story and so she wasn't aware when the girl lost interest in it. She questioned the girl about the details, who, what, when, where, why, over and over again, until she realized that the girl had begun fabricating a story to amuse her. Then this ploy bored even the girl and she either disappeared or motioned with her hand impatiently when the woman mentioned the dog. Finally, the woman felt the banality of the story, how trite, how petty it was. Her own voyeurism. The girl had only mentioned a dog in passing and the woman had closed her teeth on it like a weasel onto her prey.

If the dog itself didn't interest the girl, another part of the story did. The girl enjoyed telling stories about hunting. She came from a hunting family, she said. Or before her people had been decimated, they had been hunters and gatherers. The tradition had stayed with her, was in her blood, would be there, always. She recounted or fabricated stories about hiding, caves, traps, packs of animals, deer, mustangs, wild cats, jaguars, quetzals, wild boars, pacas, monos, jungles, snakes, wolves.

There was a series of stories of a hunter who pursued his prey from one continent to another. She had met him in Patagonia, no, in the Andes. At the Amazon, she had dared river sharks and piranha to escape him. She had seen him crossing the Himalayas, the Siberian tundra, the ice realms of Antarctica and Alaska. Lately he was settling down in the African savannahs, then he was back in the jungles of Peru. He had been everywhere and she was where he was because he was hunting her.

The girl was eloquent on the subject of the hunter. The way the animals outwitted him, the traps they laid for each other. The covey of deranged concubines who trailed the hunter, whom he had once hunted and bagged and who now egged him on. The girl's stories were montages of all stories, myths, fairy tales, she had heard and hadn't heard. They were composites of what she had read, and what she imagined, of dreams she'd had, of all the dreams she had imagined. The hunter. Sighting the hunter. The scent of the hunter. The hunter scenting his prey. The hunter tracking the girl. The magnetism of the hunter. Hunting as an erotic attraction. Tracking the hunter. Hunting him.

The hunter approached. The blue jays gave warning. The girl hid in caves. She climbed into the hollows of trees where lightning had struck. The hunter came closer. Even the wolves couldn't keep him at bay. First he found the dog. The concubines roasted it live on a spit. They ate it limb by limb, tearing it apart. Grease dripping down their chins. They buried the bones. The girl found the bones. She dug them up. She blew upon them. The dog reconstituted itself. Each time it grew larger. Still, the hunter and his harem set out hunting them again. Following the girl's canine smell. They came closer to her. They found her everywhere, anywhere.

The girl knew the animal fear of the hunter. She had the animal's knowledge of the dangerousness of guns, the animal's sense of hopelessness and despair. This information she was willing to discuss. The girl also knew the animal's power over the hunter, the animal's knowledge of the hunter's weaknesses, of the hunter's flaws. This she was not willing to discuss.

The hunter tracked her through her dreams, into night dramas. She awakened with his hands around her throat. The woman jumped to her feet from a dead sleep, running without thought of shoes or robe to the trailer which she entered in the middle of a jaguar's enraged scream; Azul was snarling and cuffing at the hands around her throat, her claws sharp, poised, stabbing. Or the jaguar was on the girl, the hunter's disguise. There were wounds on the back of her hands, along her wrists, on her forearms.

More than she could have ever imagined, the woman learned about hunters and prey, about terror and nightmare, learned what she never could have learned otherwise. But she never learned to distinguish the jaguar scream from the scream of a woman, the opening shriek that accompanied the sharp plunge of claw or fang from the scream of the prey cut to the bone, that followed.

The woman couldn't bear the girl's terror and tried to intervene, to help, in all the ways she knew but when the girl awakened, she was disdainful of the woman's efforts. The woman didn't have the strength to meet the hunter or the predators. These were the girl's nightmares and it was too dangerous to let an incompetent woman try to take them from her. She would not cease wandering in the realms of the hunter, no matter what the woman attempted.

One dawn Azul cried endlessly and soundlessly. She would say nothing. Timber entered the trailer for the first time. He moved past the woman seated by the bedside on a folding chair and climbed onto the futon, nudging the girl this way and that until he determined his own place. The girl sidled toward him and curled up into an embrace between his legs. Her head was under his muzzle, against his chest. The woman looked at the two of them and understood that she was expendable. The girl had stopped crying. She was asleep. Timber's eyes were open but he did not look at the woman. That is how quickly it happened. The woman got up wearily and left the trailer, leaving the two of them to each other. Wolf and girl were now inseparable.

Many nights, now that it was summer, the girl slept outside, fell down asleep exactly where she had been sitting or standing, and Timber, within minutes arrived beside her. "He turns me once an hour," the girl said, "to make sure that I am alive. You can set a clock by him. His cold nose, here, at my waist, and then he pushes up. I turn and he settles down on the other side of me. Do you miss him now that he's mine?"

Did she miss Timber? Long before the girl had come, when a lover had asked about Timber, the woman had said, "Timber is my mate."

The woman asked herself if she missed anything that had once belonged to her before the girl came. Her life, for example, did she miss her life? She had once had a life separate from the girl. She had once had a practice, a lover, friends, a car, a house with mortgages, bank accounts, investments, social security and tax identification numbers, telephones, answering and fax machines, credit cards, a reputation, degrees, earned and honorary, a pen name, memberships in various organizations, offices to fulfill, a motorcycle, an extensive library, subscriptions to professional and environmental magazines, box seats at the summer theatre.

Some of these still remained. Someone was caretaking this life, somehow it was being maintained, but the woman's attention was elsewhere, was where the girl was living. Sometimes she followed the girl, not, as she told herself originally, because she was concerned for the girl's welfare but because she was concerned about her own. She wanted to know how the girl found clay and the differences between the red, ochre, yellow and brown earths. She wanted to know what grasses one could eat. She watched the girl nibble the seeds of rye grass and gather the tiny green cups of miner's lettuce, or take the sweet and pungent dry pale red berries from the pepper trees, munch on the yellow mustard flowers snipping the youngest leaves on the tall stems to steam and eat with melted butter flavored with the anise which grew alongside the mustard, or graze on the sharp nasturtium flowers, red, orange, yellow, or eat rose hips, nourishing herself on the land's assortment of greens, acrid, sweet and bittersweet. It was not as if the girl had studied the mechanics of self-preservation in order to survive in a hostile world where man and animal hunted and competed against each other. It was as if the girl did not distinguish herself from what surrounded her. Walking with such a light step, she became what she took in, and submitted herself, in a series of holy offerings designed, if one could say there was a design rather than wordless and intelligent interchanges, designed to reconstitute the larger living body which breathed all things. Thinking this, the woman was grateful that she was beginning to learn to see, as Azul had instructed her, not from the outside but from the inside, but not from Azul's inside either, but from inside what the early kabbalists had called Adam Kadmon or the post-modern biologists called Gaia. Mystics in each century invented a new name for the recurring astonishment that one was simply a momentary consciousness in a great unity, the only entity one could rightly call Mind and deduced, as children did and then forgot, that the cells in one's body, the tiny atoms, the stars might also think fondly of themselves as they noted their unique and autonomous existence in otherwise dense matter. Had the girl come to this on her own? Had she been born with such an understanding, had she always been faithful to it or had circumstances, trauma being the professional term, sent her flying into space through an uppercut to the jaw, or its equivalent, returning her to this most advanced or most primitive state? Watching the girl, the woman was constantly teetering between one conviction or the other, enlightenment on the one hand, madness or injury on the other, and not being able to find any confirmation through either observation or insight, she found herself dizzy as one gets when realizing that one is on a tightrope and can seriously injure oneself by falling in either direction. Or rather, no matter what, a fall is inevitable.

There was, she saw, an essential difference between herself and the girl. The girl loved being outdoors and only came inside when the need to hibernate or cocoon herself took over, or at the woman's insistence, or when she was fatigued from wind or rain or the summer's intense heat. The woman loved the outdoors and never went out. She was afraid. The great love she bore for the outdoors frightened her. The love was frightening. Also the pleasure. The more beautiful it was, the more intense her joy, the more alarmed she felt, the more quickly she gathered herself up and took herself inside. Locked the door. Watched the birds through the windows like a prisoner longing to be free.

So she followed the girl. Or not quite. She walked in the girl's tracks. She went out when the girl came in, or walked east after the girl had returned and was walking west toward the sunset. She didn't want to come upon the girl without warning, didn't want to intrude in her space, she didn't want to know where she was. She only wanted to know where she had been, where the past lived, had hidden itself like spores waiting for the end of a long, benighted human season.

Timber did not return to be with the woman, he did not walk with the woman as he had when she, in the past, had "taken hikes," her way of being outdoors that had a healthy intent and so fit in with the life the woman had been living, or thought she was required to live. Now Timber stayed close to the girl.

But, he vouched for the woman, that she was, as she claimed, trustworthy, that she knew more about freedom than her life indicated, that she would fight for it in others even when she didn't know how to achieve it for herself. That contrary to her appearance, the woman was feisty and honorable.

This was, after all, the woman who had taken the leash from his collar within days of their moving to the canyon. She had refused to keep him behind fences. When he had lusted for the motley bitch in heat who was confined in an unused outhouse for the duration of "her time," he had attacked the door, had broken the latch, had freed the skinny wreck of an obsequious mutt who had slunk out of her container like someone whose crime, best disguised, was her liveliness. He had mounted her to inject freedom in her progeny if not into her, and had withstood forever, for her, and her litter, and her litter's litters, the humiliation of her keeper's turning a cold hose on both of them with the thought of impeding the necessity of the gene pool or of assisting her in disentangling herself from her attachment to the spike of his cock, the burr, the thorn which was lodged in her the way foxtails would enter his own skin in order to hitch a ride to wherever they thought they were going. When Timber had done this, the woman had stood by him.

The neighbor was distraught. Her wolf, he had fumed, had trespassed on his property and had broken down the door of his dog house and had violated the bitch. What was the woman going to do about this?

What indeed could the woman do? She had thought of offering to have the mutt spayed and the litter destroyed in the process, but she rather favored the idea of the swayback mongrel with cocker ears and a Dalmatian body birthing wolf pups with hackles rising. She could explain that he wasn't her wolf, that wolves just didn't, couldn't, belong to anyone.

"I'll talk to him," she had said solemnly. "I don't know if he will consider his behavior aggressive or untoward, but I will explain the situation to him and ask him to cease and desist." She hung up the phone before the man recovered from his splutter and fluster. And she did talk with Timber. They had had a long heart to heart about human nature, rules, laws, expectations, property, territory and about wolf nature, laws, territory, etc. Timber didn't say so explicitly, but he seemed to favor natural law over human law and could find little common ground with the neighbor in the area of property. Timber knew quite well what belonged to him, what he was responsible for, what he had to protect within the marked boundaries of his territory, not less than he could survey, not more than he needed to hunt and sustain himself and his pack, the woman included. He knew who were his mates, what he owed to them. The pups, as it turned out, were far cuter than any the mongrel might have had with the other mutts in the neighborhood. The woman's neighbor sold them for a good price instead of giving them away to anyone who would have them. Afterwards, he had her spayed. The door was never repaired on the out-house and Timber had no interest in a fixed female who sent very few signals over the airwaves.

"You were pretty brazen with the neighbor," Azul commented one morning as a way of thanking the woman for hanging in with her. The woman assumed that Azul was privy to some of the gossip in the neighborhood and had pieced a story together from the rag pile.

"Do you miss Timber now that he's mine?" Azul insisted on an answer.

"I have you," the woman said with a quiver.

The woman who had been watching the girl began watching the two of them together, studying their voiceless camaraderie. When it was too much for her, she retreated to her garden, trimming the roses and the vines, weeding and mulching among the calla lilies. She had always loved their white petals unfolding around the golden center for their bold purity, but dreaded their unavoidable fate, the slight puckering of the white petals foreshadowing inescapable imperfection. She cut them the moment she noticed the slightest brown stain. She mourned the wolf in a whirl of pollen, honey and decay.

Timber had made the land his by virtue of marking the territory through scent and through habit. He claimed it as assertively as humans claimed the land, and as they were oblivious to his rights, he disdained theirs. The woman watched him teeter before a fence going up here, a garage there, concrete over earth, lawn replacing sage, until he found his way again, constructing and marking other paths through and around his territory. As time went on, he stayed closer to home and was satisfied because she lived at the end of the road, because she had not put up many fences, because the developed land slid into the far wilder park land at the edge of her patio, into stands of scrub oak, and fields of coyote bush, chamisa, the girl called it, and also lupine, catnip, bush monkey flower, cow parsnip that tumbled toward horsetails and cattails along the creeks.

At home, there had once been places one might always find him, alongside the woman's bed, against the chaise on the boundary between rooms, under the oleanders, which had become a wall ten feet long and fifteen feet high, most often covered with white blossoms, in a dug out cave under the roots of an oak at the crest of the knoll, in the arched doorway of the neighbor's house, not the one with the silly bitch he had tried to rescue, but the house of a family who lived with an old and cranky brown lab who was slow and sweetly devoted to him, a hausfrau of a dog, a housecoat, an apron of an animal. Timber had added the trailer and under the trailer to these locations and was there most often, watching the girl from outside if she was inside, accompanying the girl as she wandered, waiting for her if she had driven away. If the woman hadn't continued to feed him, she wondered if he would have returned to her — their

— house at all.

"Don't you ever want to sleep in my — in this — house?" Sometimes the girl did, but always on the floor and never again, as she had the first night, on the bed, and then only if Timber was willing to lay down beside her as if he were either her beloved or her bodyguard.

The girl was never there in the morning, awakening as she did, before dawn so that she could be outside with the morning creatures greeting the sunrise, and so the ritual of drifting off together into the night mattered a great deal to the woman who might not see the girl for the entire day or days on end, unless the girl needed her. In need, Azul came into the house on her own, or climbed the pepper tree and whistled plaintively, or lay down across the threshold, or sent Timber to fetch the woman, or simply cried out sharply day or night like a bird watching a snake sidle away with a blue egg in its mouth. What gave the woman joy was holding Azul's hand as they both drifted off to sleep. Or being asked for a story, a variation always on the same story, the one about the iguana that — who — as she had been instructed, the woman was gradually coming to know. The story invariably appeared in a drawing every time the woman told a new version of it:

"The iguana, who had no language, had music. When he spoke, that is when he moved his mouth though nothing issued from it, not even breath, a sound appeared, a bell in the tree, a whistle among the manzanitas, a gong in the apricot tree, chimes in the jade plants. The music was no ordinary music, it was as much color as it was melody. All the sounds had a shade, a tint, a hue. They shimmered in the air, fluorescent against the leaves or sky.

"The bell had a blue sound, azulado, shivering into purple the way the mist below the mountain turns azure against ice dark peaks when the sky during certain late summer sunsets flares dangerously with the color of salamanders. The gong was a deep orange that broached the variations of comets streaking across the blackest night and the chimes were the night dark of the woods, the blue peal of spruce and the ring of small dusky blue juniper berries. The small, sharp silver whistle of the olive trees and the startling white chorus of the aspen bark, piercing as snow falling against sunset in the late afternoon."

Azul did not want story in the usual sense. Any evocation of plot, drama, character, she hadn't herself defined, alarmed her. She had created a world where she was safe and she didn't allow anyone, even the woman, to intercede in it. She wanted variations on sound and color. Perhaps, the woman reflected, this was the way she saw and experienced the world now. Her work had taught the woman that individuals experienced the world differently, that they organized it into different shapes and categories. Awareness was not uniform and this was the reason that individuals perceived beauty and safety in their own ways.

More than anything, the woman was aware that beauty didn't arise on its own, was not self-propagating. Beauty, by its nature, evolved out of or within relationship. The harmony intrinsic to beauty required call and response for the reconciliation of the parts that would afterwards take one's breath away. It didn't matter if it was the burnt red sap of the eucalyptus streaming toward its root or the sweet burden of jasmine releasing into moon-sweet night, or the girl's own startling loveliness. Her innocence in the midst of horror, a demeanor essentially untainted, untaintable despite blows and ravishment, a constant and recurring rejuvenation of grateful delight, called forth language to meet it eye to eye.

"What else?" the girl asked snuggling into the woman. The girl's head was in her lap as the woman was stroking her hair gently and then whispering into her ear the story of the iguana who had come to live — the woman spoke softly wanting the story to make the girl happy — along the curve around the girl's ear.

It had taken a long time for the iguana to make his home here, to find a nest in the secret space where he could be invisible and present at the same time. The woman traced the place where the iguana lived, the grip of his feet on the edge of the ear, the head tucked over the side and resting in the soft circle which was the entrance to sound. She tapped her finger gently at the entrance to the inner ear and the girl smiled.

"At night when the girl was even stiller than she was in the day, the iguana rose on his four feet and puffed himself up..."

"The iguana rose on her four feet and puffed herself up..." Azul said.

And the woman accommodated immediately. "The iguana rose on her four feet and puffed herself up, transparent blue against the green lines of her body and breathed her secret into the girl's dreams. The girl learned the language she was to learn. She took on the knowledge and with it the charge of protecting the knowledge. She never told anyone what she knew. She only practiced the knowledge in order not to forget it. In the middle of the woods, in the middle of the night when no humans were around, she sang the silent song of the iguana and the woods came alive with color and light."

In the morning, she noticed a unique motionlessness in the girl squatting on the cement by the woodpile, the way an animal freezes in order to become invisible by diminishing the distinction between organic and inorganic, by slowing everything, time within and time without, so that the creature cannot be differentiated from stone or sand. Even from behind, the woman was certain that the girl's eyes were wide open and unblinking, that the girl was in a state of motionless alert and knowing this the woman had her first conscious experience of predatory mind which can see clearly through the disguise of circumstances so that it can, like a heron, stab a fish through murky water. The girl was making infinitesimally small movements inclining her head so slowly, you couldn't believe she had turned 90 degrees and was facing the woodpile. Timber, as was his habit, was sleeping calmly a few feet away under the oleander bush but she was not talking to Timber. To herself, then. To no one. And then she lifted her open palm toward herself and brought it toward her mouth. Her other hand moved across her palm with gentle strokes.

Knowing the woman was there, the girl turned and walked, again in slow motion, toward the woman and kneeled down next to her, her palm open like a leaf on which a small creature, wondering about the miracle of traveling through space, was perched. "This is Yerba Buena Verde," she said, stroking a lizard marked with tones of green with one finger as it rested on her palm as if it was a leaf. Her lover is Romero Azulito. He is bluer."

The next day the woman found a green scroll wrapped in tin foil and tied with a gold ribbon. The girl had drawn her own face as if she were a jungle of gold and black, sunlight and wet bark. It is not easy to draw one's own profile, to understand one's own face in repose and from such a distance and angle. The profile of the girl against a view of a woods was at the same time all the animals and birds arranged in a pattern so that the outline of one body became the outline of another. The girl's eye was open staring at the animals and around her ear was an iguana and from its mouth came a breath of musical notes. The name of the drawing was, "The first iguana invents Quechua."

Much to her own inner embarrassment, the woman was damned proud of this event. She was unable to stop herself from feeling that she had achieved something with the girl, had offered her safety, land, location and so, in a small way, was making amends for land taken, dislocation, danger.

And had she, she wondered, as she watched the girl, or the shadow of the girl, or glimpses of the girl, the way she watched clouds changing in the sky, taking one shape and metamorphosing into another, had she ever in her life brought healing to anyone or anything before? This was not an invited question. It was a self-centered, therefore rude and defiant question before which everything she had constructed teetered like a hut built of sticks, collapsing. That's a sentimental and melodramatic question, a wiser inner voice suggested. She pursued it stubbornly: Had she ever in her life healed anything? She didn't want to belittle her work but she didn't want to step away from the truth either.

If I could heal one thing, one person...?

The woman officially gave up her therapeutic practice for the summer. It didn't stop her from seeing her former patients, it only stopped her from thinking about them as patients and inspired her, instead, to invite them to visit with her as "guests" since this was the title the girl had given them and that she had accepted. Earlier she had said she was going to take a long vacation, was going to travel. She had believed this. She would never have allowed herself to stop working and stay home. But now she said, she was staying home to take care of the girl. Something was different but her friends couldn't tell what it was. They expected to find the house a mess, but it wasn't. It seemed to be in disarray but actually everything was arranged even more neatly than before. A re-arrangement of space. The interposition of silence. Subtle order created through emptiness.

It was all confusing to the woman but the confusion was engaging. In the manner of a Zen koan, bafflement calmed her. She told herself that the wild had come to her, but she had to admit that she didn't know what wild meant. She had thought wild meant a heavy yellow creature springing on her shoulders from behind, claws extended. She had thought it had meant teeth in her neck. She had thought it meant lightning, sulfur, wildfires. She had found such danger thrilling. Exotic. It would make a woman of her, she had imagined. She had never dreamed this, the girl's soft fingers along the spine of Yerba Buena. The feathers of the girl drifting down upon her from her downy breast.

Her friends rarely saw the girl. She would run when she heard a car. She was always barefoot, unobtrusive, and could disappear, could transform like a salamander. Always present. Invisible.

Their life had become, the woman slowly found words and with words understanding, a marriage between the seen and the unseen. She had waited a lifetime for this. This was a surprising thought for a woman who had a lover.

"If you could heal one person, Owl Woman, shouldn't it be yourself?" Azul never failed to startle the woman. "If one could heal one thing, should one start with oneself?" Eenie meenie miney mo, catch a lizard by the toe.... Who should it be? Yerba Buena Verde was on the girl's palm as she had been for weeks, it seemed, lowering her miniature dragon's head to the girl's soft and continuous stroke. Timber followed stiffly behind and waited patiently for the girl to lay the lizard down and attend him, and behind them all, actually, or, in her mind, the woman followed also stroking, caressing, soothing. Such a retinue.

"Shouldn't it be yourself?" Wasn't she healed? Wasn't she healed sufficiently to heal others? What did Azul understand that had bypassed psychotherapy? An essential part of the woman's training had centered on her own healing and it was presumed that the work had been effective and she could proceed to work with others. Now it seemed that her training itself might be what needed to be healed and that the woman was not alone in her suffering, but her entire profession, almost everyone she knew was suffering similarly.

Azul's presence continuously threw the woman into a quandary. The woman had believed that healing is possible, that she had been healed from whatever she suffered from her past, as everyone suffers their past, and so she could extend healing to others. Her profession and her training accorded her that skill.

But Azul seemed to be healing by virtue of living so resolutely in a world she was choosing and inventing. Azul seemed to be healing by consciously changing her life, living according to what made sense to her. Azul's relationship with Yerba Buena Verde was critical. Yerba Buena Verde and Timber were her healers.

The woman had assumed she had been healed from her afflictions when she was functioning capably in the social construction that was called the public world. One day she had awakened from a nightmare, recorded it dutifully but with little affect, propelled by curiosity not pain, tussled briefly with the more elusive meanings of the obscure images and had gone to the office where she attended several other nightmares not of her own making. She accompanied her patients in expressing, examining, understanding their pain until it was necessary to confine it in an airtight container which could be opened or closed at will until they met again. That day it was confirmed that the woman had come through a wormhole from a bitter past into a manageable and more hopeful present. Reflecting now on her personal and professional history, she recognized she had faced any number of unspeakable events, had faced innumerable demons, had scrutinized thousands of real or imagined horrors and memories, had wept, grieved, lamented, raged, writhed, wailed, calmed, interpreted, understood, forgiven, had, within the permitted hour or hours, deconstructed and reconstructed first a self and then a life without ever daring to make the most obvious and most simple statement: This life, all the lives lived under these circumstances, are not worth living. The profound systemic injuries to all life had not been the focus of her education, training, or healing. She had not been authorized to help people recognize the horrific circumstances that enveloped them.

Honesty required the woman to admit to herself that she still had her own nightmares which had long preceded the girl and the lover, but she didn't speak to the girl about them. She dealt with them in the old ways in which she had been trained. She dutifully stalked their symbolic equivalents in her daily life and in her history. It had never occurred to her before that they might be autonomous, might have their own life, that she had to meet them as real beings on their own territory if there was going to be any resolution. So, learning from Azul, she began searching out her own images and her own nightmare geography.

The third rail of the subway. Sparks flying. Vast dump sites smoldering. Endless landscapes of twisted fenders, greasy, bent, rusted, unserviceable automobile parts. Miles of cracked plastic tubing. Storm clouds of plastic bags wafted by fierce winds. Mangled rubber hoses. Cities collapsed into endless miles of sewers. The woman was always lost in deserted subway stations, stairs going down and then down again and then down again.

Trying to find her way through labyrinths of dull mirrors whose undersides, chipped silver backing, reflected faint and grotesque images. Cities of the lost. Unimaginable cruelty and violence. Torture. Bombs and landmines. Bundles of quivering rags. Abandoned infants passed from smudged and empty breast to smudged and empty breasts. Herself dissolving at each dead end as she stooped to rescue a radioactive tar baby which expired in a pouf of smoke. Ashes.

What was turning to ash in her own life? That was a stupid and solipsistic question. The girl said she was in mourning for the world even though everyone — the woman included — whom Azul had ever encountered had tried to convince her that her suffering was personal, that it was her story alone, only her own story that was making her suffer. The girl said that dreams were not personal and came to anyone who would carry them. Those who would take them on, remembered them. The rest said they didn't dream.

At this, the girl's mouth turned up in sorrow and sounded an inaudible mournful night cry intending to incite the coyotes to jabber their own hopeless lament that would be answered, in turn, by a thousand disappeared creatures punctuated by shrill, hopeless canine whimpers from behind locked doors. No more night owl cries, no answers from night hawks, no bats soaring through the night trees. Informed by the ways that animals declare themselves within the domain of the subsonic, the girl invoked innumerable silences in a conversation which ultimately included everything consigned to the missing and the unnamed. This was the lament that the woman had first heard from the girl, the aria which had drawn her forth to the base of the tree, had rooted her to the spot, incorporating her in an unexpected, unprecedented alliance with the mute and the hounded. Before the woman could even consider meeting the particular images for which she, clearly, was being given responsibility, in short — macadam ruins netted in landslides of rebar and iron netting — she prayed they would not bury her until she had been able to secure the happiness of the girl.

"You don't understand anything yet," the girl declared.

That afternoon the girl came back to visit the woman and sat in the woman's chair indicating that the woman should sit on the couch. The girl made herself a cup of chocolate, finely grating the chocolate and brought one for the woman herself.

"What are you thinking?" the woman asked. The girl had been unsuccessful in weaning her from the word.

"I was wondering what I was seeing behind your eyes."

Tears welled up immediately. Tears she hadn't known were there.

"Behind the tears," the girl said.

"I don't know," the woman answered somewhat truthfully.

"I can't talk to you until you find out," the girl said.

"What difference does it make?"

"I thought we were friends," the girl said matter-of-factly.

"I'll find out," the woman said.

"I can help you," the girl said. "I know about such things."

"And then what?" the woman asked as she watched everything she had tried to set up as protection crumble between them.

"And then we'll really be friends."

"What good will I be to you then?"

"Be real," Azul said with irritation, getting up from the chair. "I don't want to know your secrets. And I certainly don't think I can fix anything. I just want you to be real."

The girl left and Timber went with her. She left behind an ultimate challenge: The girl wanted to be friends. The woman remained on the couch, realizing that moving to her chair would change the dynamic she was being called to enter. The woman had been taught to put up a wall between friendship and healing. What did the woman know about friendship or healing if she believed she had to leave herself out of each of them for the sake of the other person? The girl wanted to be friends. That wasn't quite it. The girl hoped the woman would appreciate the value of friendship between them.

She almost called the girl back. She almost said, "I need you." She almost admitted she was lost. She almost admitted she was frightened. She almost got up and made herself another cup of chocolate. What were her secrets after all? The girl had come into her house naked for God's sake!

The phone rang. It was a "guest." "How are you, my dear?" she said in what sounded to her like a sufficiently warm and professional, but admittedly, false voice. By the time she finished the conversation, she had pulled herself together even more.

I t was raining. Hard. The woman saw the girl in the tree and was alarmed because the lightning was drawing nearer. She ran out as she still had a tendency to do and admonished the girl for not taking care of herself. She would catch a cold. She would be injured.

The girl turned a deaf ear to the woman's entreaties and the woman was pushed to the edge of her dark warnings. "You'll be struck by lightning." The woman felt jagged fear sear through her.

"I've experienced worse," the girl said. "But I don't think I will be struck by lightning."

"How can you be so sure? What kind of madness is that?"

"The tree will take the lightning down to the ground."

"How do you know that?"

"Don't you know trees, Owl Woman?"

"Don't you know trees?" the woman repeated scornfully. "Is there something in the physiology of trees that will protect you from lightning when you're in one while the defenseless tree may go up in smoke?"

"There is something in this tree which will protect me. Or, it will let me know I should get down."

"Do you want me to believe that the tree is in cahoots with you?"

"Yes," the girl said.

"And you want me to act as if you're not crazy."

"Yes," the girl said, "since I extend to you the courtesy that you're not ignorant and your mind is not as limited as it sometimes seems. I can't always be sure if the tree is talking to me, but often it is."

"You won't come down, then."

"No."

"Because you want to prove to me that you're not crazy."

"No, because I want to be here."

"This makes me feel crazy," the woman shouted.

"I'm sorry," the girl said. "The truth is you do look like a crazy woman standing in the rain, with so much water running down your face, shouting at me. Why don't you go in the house, get dry, make yourself a cup of chamomile tea and calm down. By that time, the storm will be over and I'll come in and see if you are feeling better."

It was hopeless. She stomped into the house. There was nothing she could do to protect the girl from herself.

She made a cup of tea. Suddenly, the girl's advice made sense. She made another cup of tea for the girl and brought it to her.

"The lightning is very far away now," the girl said. "Sit down under the tree if you like and enjoy the fine rain on your body. You'll feel much better out here than under that ugly roof that cuts you off from the elements."

"I've never noticed that the roof is ugly."

"Because you're never outside. Because you don't sit here or haven't gone up to the top of the hill and looked down on it. When I got to the top the first time, I had to find another place to stand so I wouldn't see it. Tar paper, patches of tar, pipes sticking out. It's a mess. When I'm up in the tree I have to face away. Pity the poor birds, Owl Woman."

There was something birdlike about the girl. The way she was moving her head. Quick, stiff gestures. A woodpecker moved in her, swiveled her head in tiny horizontal increments from side to side. Then a blue jay, more cautious, alert, suspicious making even smaller quicker movements, head down, up, cocked, turning, cocked again and again and again.

The girl saw that she was making the woman sad. She relented. "Come out here. Sit down here. Don't be afraid." The girl threw down a damp pillow she had been protecting in a plastic bag. The woman didn't know what else to do and so she did as she was told. She would have liked to think she was doing what the girl was suggesting, but it wasn't true, she was doing what she was told. The woman couldn't yet admit to herself that Azul's position in the tree offered a certain startling intelligence. Call it point of view. Call it outlook. Call it perspective.

The woman didn't need to be up in the tree in order to benefit from it. She needed, she admitted now to herself, her ass on the bare ground and the tree at her back. She left the plastic covered pillow to the side. A myriad ugly expressions came to mind: "Get your ass out here." Or even from her grandmother, the Yiddish, "Tuchus aufen tish — Put your ass on the table" — which ambivalently valorized what the grandmother considered a certain peasant intelligence about forthrightness. She breathed deeply, taking in the breath of the tree. Asylum. It happened in stages; she abandoned herself to the girl first, then to the tree and finally, most belatedly, to herself. The rain came heavy again. A warm rain.

She was repeating the donkey phrases in her mind when she came upon the magic spell, "You're an ass." There was a story she had loved when she was young though it had also embarrassed her to love it so much and so she had only read it when no one else was around and had never ever asked to have it read aloud.

There was a young man who, for reasons she didn't remember now and which hadn't ever mattered to her, had eaten cabbages from a field only to discover that the leaves of one variety of cabbage would turn him into an ass while the delicate leaves of another kind liberated him from the enchantment. The ass, she had learned long before she had formally studied mythology in order to understand the psyche, had been worshipped as a god in ancient Egypt, highly honored then demonized in an everyday inter-god squabble. Set, the dry principle, lord of the desert and everything that dry heat preserves was always at war with the ultimate decay of Osiris the robust compost god of vegetation. Set was an ass, as was ass-eared Midas, as was Pales for whom Palestine was named, and not to forget the golden ass of Apuleius, or Hannah the Hebrew Matriarch who had found wild asses in the desert which became essential to the people's survival, or that Samson had defeated the Philistines with the jaw bone of an ass, nor to forget that Christ had ridden into Jerusalem on an ass. Then there was Balaam's ass, the best of all because he could see the angel when Balaam couldn't. Clearly, the woman still resembled Balaam more than the ass.

She was up against one of those conundrums that never failed to dizzy her after which, whenever she found her own ground, she was oddly comforted by understanding that she was getting closer to the wrong side, closer to taking a very uncivilized view by remaining faithful to the animal and the sacred, by failing to separate one from the other, and being unwilling to give up what she always thought was a better story if you took it seriously.

Frankly, what had always puzzled her was only that cabbages were merely cabbages, cole slaw was only cole slaw, sauerkraut was merely sauerkraut, cabbage leaves were not delicate, they were a plain and poor food, with or without corned beef. Why, indeed, had Rapunzel's mother longed so desperately for those growing in the witch's garden? Why had the cabbages which the young man ingested made such a sweet and enticing salad?

As a child, the woman had tended the inner field of cabbages in her mind with great care and attention, knowing which species grew where, coveting the stolen moments when she could take on the muddy view of princesses who passionately loved donkeys, remembering in detail all the stories of donkeys and donkey skins, beauty hidden under hides, donkey musicians, enchanted or not, lute players all of them.

It had been the process of metamorphosis that had fascinated her; demanding that she gnaw on the wrong cabbages until her ears turned long as corn stalks and silky rough with fine short gray corn hairs, until she could really hear for the first time the song of birds and the complex conversations between them. So intriguing was the creature world of music she would enter, she did not mind her arms elongating, her hands shortening into hooves, her mouth and nose extending into muzzle, from which, she was convinced, she could make glorious sounds if only allowed to practice long enough. When it had been time to eat the right cabbage and leave her animal because her mother was calling her, because there were chores to do, because her real life was calling to her and would not accept her deep throaty musical bray as an answer, she always moved back across the threshold of her imagination with great reluctance, stubborn as an ass.

Yes, this was the story through which, as a child, she first glimpsed the distressing truth that the allegedly wise were often unable to recognize the face of the holy and so assumed it was a disguise and disparaged it or ridiculed it or, worse, persecuted it, hunted it down, killed it. Inevitably, the holy disappeared.

Maybe it was the effect of the lightning, ozone on her brain that was leading the woman into an electric reverie of disguised princes and princesses, escaping the clutches of royal courts and monarchs for forest refuges. She was retreating to the forests in a donkey hide, more lithe and luxurious than any armor or velvet robe, or hooped ball gowns of jewel-studded satin might be. What she feared was that she would be ferreted out of her idyll, forced to yield up her animal skins to the fire, to take on the prison of human identity in exchange for some gold coins, a set of silver dishes, an unending supply of wine and merry drunkenness, a castle with a barnyard and stable but without a single singing donkey. She was afraid she would have to endure until her death the tedium of a royal marriage, the wearying responsibilities of royal rule. This is the fate the girl was trying to save her from as if the girl knew that the woman had always been overwhelmed by anxiety, disappointment and terror when she had come upon these terrible moments in fairy tales.

Cabbages, asses, music had taken her then as the memory of them did now, as she sat, more comfortably than she could have imagined, under the tree where the birds were silent in the rain.

The woman moved closer to the trunk. The girl's body was partially shielding her from the rain. Everything the woman had ever thought flowed away into silver rivulets that trickled down the trunk from the leaves into the earth. Under the leaves in the uppermost branches, a few small birds were gathered for shelter. This is how still we have become, the woman noticed gratefully.

There was a gift in appearances. Leaning back against the tree, her face lifted tentatively to the now soft drizzle, she felt secure that her expression communicated peacefulness. Hard won but authentic tranquility. Under this disguise, she let her memories run amuck. Summer camp. A storm. Washing her hair in the rain hoping the deluge would last through the shampoo and rinse. It did. She had been wet, washed, thoroughly and still the water pinged down onto the wooden porch.

A hurricane. She had warned her mother who had not listened. Then her mother had had to carry her on her back, waist deep in water, to their house which was, fortunately, two stories, the first story set seven steps high above a basement.

When she had first moved to her present house, an African lion had escaped from a local animal park absurdly situated in a suburban neighborhood. She had cheered the animal as he made his way across the lawns and boulevards, through shrubs and hedges, up into the foothills and then, miraculously, into the vast park itself where he survived a few days. He was safe there, having had little competition for the ample and protected game, until he was hunted down. School children arrived in yellow buses, wearing yellow slickers, to watch the pursuit as a little army of police dogs and dog catchers, an unlikely alliance if there ever was one, followed his wet trail in the steady rain up to Eagle Rock where he was cornered finally by a shallow cave, shot with a tranquilizer gun and returned to his cage. Oh, how the woman had cheered it on, had prayed that the posse would could lose the scent, and he would outwit the trackers and make a lonely but contented life or ally himself with a pack of mountain lionesses and spawn tawny half-breed cubs that would lounge in summer on the hot boulders at the peaks of the dry hills.

The wild was a dream and only a dream, she admitted to herself. An imagined state of mind which made her woozy with metaphor and heightened passion. She was working hard enough simply sitting in the rain, a far cry from becoming a woman who knew and honored the ways of great cats, protected their turf from herself and her own kind, or who gave up everything to live among them without endangering or inhibiting them in the least.

"Do you think I'm doing you harm?" she called up to the girl.

"Quiet and don't fidget so," the girl whispered so softly that her voice was no more than the shushing of the breeze. "You'll startle the birds who have more right to be here than you. This is their house, you know, and you have somewhere else to go, but they don't." The woman hadn't felt a single muscle twitch while the girl had felt the tremors of her mind as if they were the plates under the earth adjusting themselves against each other.

The wild was coming close, the woman was thinking. Whatever it was that she had been taught was dangerous but which she still longed for, or thought she did, was approaching; she could hear the inaudible crack of small branches under the stealthy tread of invisible creatures. For some people, even the presence of deer was alarming and so they built fences higher and higher to prevent the creatures from leaping over their boundaries. Yes, most of her neighbors were disturbed by the small and gentle mice, rabbits and raccoon. As for herself, she didn't want them in the house, that was true; she didn't want them in the house yet; that was truer. She hadn't wanted anyone in the house, had furnished it with a zen-like sparseness, valuing silence, emptiness, space, distance, independence. Now, she missed the girl when the girl kept to herself or slept on the land or went off singing with Timber.

Her bottom was wet and cold. Water dribbled down the plastic covering on the pillow next to her with the rest of the water running down her body, settling under her. The girl, like the birds, was singing now that the rain paused, a thin melodious warble which rose to meet the steaming colors of the plants, wet, deep, vibrant against the rain dark sky. No rainbow except for the girl's melody and the way it parted into different tones as she addressed first one bird and then another.

"I know what you're thinking, Owl Woman."

"You couldn't."

Azul trilled in answer, the sound both enticing and mocking, both of those, at the same time. The woman could answer or not, though through her choice she would know which response the sonorous twitter represented.

"You don't trust me," the girl speculated.

"That's out of left field," the woman countered.

"I doubt it," the girl was attached to her certainties.

"I don't trust me," the woman offered.

"Home run."

"Every time I say something there are consequences."

"Sounds like the kind of wisdom you would give me. No surprise it works for you, too. What is it, Owl Woman?"

"I was remembering a moment, a very small moment really. Well, maybe not small so much as the kind of moment one tells as an exotic story when one returns from a trip, and so defuses it." The girl was listening in a way that told the woman that she would be heard, a gift she had extended to others for years but she wasn't used to being on the receiving end. "To tell you the truth, I must have spoken about this in that way, trying to keep the memory and distance myself from it at the same time. I don't really know why I'm thinking about it now except I want to change my relationship to the story. Do you want to hear about it?"

"Yes, I do."

And she did, it seemed to the woman for she was still now, the way she was still with lizards and sweetly attentive.

"It's about the trip I took to Kenya when I was a delegate to the UN Conference on Women. Not the official conference, but the pre-conference of non-governmental organizations. We were there to talk about peace. Most of us were women and we really wanted to talk about peace. When the official conference began, with many more male delegates, most of us left. We didn't want to listen to a lot of rhetoric, official speeches, such like. The Kenyan government offered us a tour of the surrounding areas. Maybe they wanted to get us troublemakers out of town. A group of us signed up. After we'd been on the bus for some hours, I noticed an aboriginal woman from Australia sitting by herself in the back. She was a large dark woman wearing a pale blue dress with puffy sleeves trimmed with white lace that had bound her large arms so tightly, she had, deliberately, it was clear, opened some of the seams. It was a little girl's dress and she was a very large woman. It was incongruous, a dress someone must have given to her when trying to imagine what proper dress might be for such a function.

I wanted to know her and I didn't have any idea how to go about it. Why did I want to know her? Because she was different? Was I romanticizing the other, engaging in a fantasy of the exotic? Or was it real, did I really want to know her? Do you know what I mean, Azul? Well, I could have spent the entire trip cross-examining myself to understand my motives so I decided to trust myself, assuming I wouldn't do too much harm, and got up from sitting with my colleagues and slipped into the seat next to her. Now there was the question of language or accent — she couldn't understand me and I couldn't understand her. We hardly spoke because the first exchanges were awkward and she did not seem inclined to engage in a conversation. She sat with her eyes pressed against the glass window which we couldn't open. It was obvious that I'd changed my seat, so what did I want from her? Who knows what she thought. After about an hour, she almost turned toward us but keeping her face against the glass called out "Giraffe," pointing to where it was. I didn't see anything. She took my hand and placed my finger in the right position on the glass for me to focus my eyes. No luck. I took up my binoculars, as did everyone in the bus, but we couldn't see anything. Then, minutes later, there, against the far mountains, something moving, a shadow against the raised earth. "Three," she said, "no, five. They're feeding from the tree." Later on it was the same: elephants, wildebeests, zebras.

"She saw them all. Before the guide, before any of us spotted them.

"I thought about this for a long time. In fact, I've never stopped thinking about it. Almost every day. It was seven years ago. Whenever I'm alone and look out the window, I wonder, what am I incapable of seeing? What would it take to learn to see like that? And why don't I try to learn? It's not a question of eyesight, you understand."

"I know that."

"You see that way. Did you work on it?"

"Oh no. I was born with it. But, if I didn't have it from the beginning, I think I would have worked at it. I would have wanted it.

"Anything else?" Azul asked as if she knew there was something else.

"This is more confusing. The same day, we came to a Masai compound. They took us into their ritual hut — dung roof and dung walls. Earth floor. We sat with them. Other buses came. Other women descended. There were no common languages between us. I heard English, French, Japanese, Russian, Shona, Arabic.

"We were shown a model building. The people acted as if they were very proud. Gray cinder blocks. A cement floor. The water was puddling on the slab which was already stained before it was anywhere near completion. The iron poles were rusting. A half finished building already in decay. There were lots of flies there too. We went back into our buses."

"Is that it?"

"Yes."

"Is that when you took those photographs with the Masai women?"

"Yes."

"Are you sorry?"

"Yes."

"Are you sad?"

"Yes."

"Are you wet?"

"Yes, but that's not the problem."

"I understand because I used to make stained glass windows until I asked why look through glass to see the sky. I once designed a church that only had the frames for the glass but not the glass. I wanted to put in an earth floor with different herbs under the pews so the scent would rise whenever anyone kneeled down and ... well, you know. I wanted .... I had a lot of ideas but they wanted the glass I had designed because I'd found a way they could change the colors themselves by sliding different panes into the vaulted ceiling and I said I had changed my mind and...."

There had been a life then, a real life, the woman was thinking, with commissions and responsibilities and contracts and then...?

"Doesn't matter, Owl Woman, doesn't matter." The pause was just long enough for the distant storm to refract the light so that the hill surrounding them became for one instant the girl's stained glass windows and in that time the frown that had darkened the girl's face first deepened and then disappeared too. "You know I really like sleeping outside on the earth. Would you like to join me?"

"No, that's not what's making me sad."

"What is it then?"

"That I don't know."

"What?"

"I don't know anything."

"I think that's a good thing, Owl Woman. And I don't love you less. It's such a burden, all your knowing. It makes me tired." She was climbing down the tree now and squatted directly before the woman picking up her hand and sniffing it. "Sandalwood."

If she had had her wits about her, the woman would have protested the girl curling up in her lap which meant, of course, that the white dress was saturated with mud and both of them were filthy, but she had laid her wits aside exactly as Azul had been instructing her, and that meant that she could pull the girl toward her, wrapping her arms around her, trying to warm the girl with the warmth that, since the girl had come into her domain, consistently emanated from her body.

There were two owls who lived by their house. Their house. This was the first time the woman had thought that. Cafélatté and Chocolatté. The girl had named them. The names amused the woman, "These names are very amusing to Tecolote," she said aloud, looking into the mirror, wondering how she would look when she was old, when her round owl eyes would stare out of a face whose flesh was receding from her bones, a face flattened like the owls and then sharpened like the raptors, hawk, falcon, and eagle. People grow into their names, their faces take on the meanings attributed to them earlier. She would become a bird, the girl had sealed her fate; it was as certain as any christening. Accordingly, she began watching the owls at night, learning to discern their dark shapes on the telephone pole, alerted by the first hoot of one to the other. She did not understand the owls yet. They hovered on wires, at the tops of the high trees, scanning the ground for field mice and other small creatures. They were awfully silent but when then the woman was attempting to learn such stillness from them, they hooted. As if to warn their prey. As if to give notice of danger. Decency and fairness the woman couldn't imagine.

"Cafélatté and Chocolatté will make their home here forever," the girl announced with her usual feathery certainty, "forever with you my very, very dear Tecolote." Something had changed indeed.

And so could change again. The woman had no sooner begun thinking of the owls in the tree when the girl brought home road kills, two owls that she had found within several miles on the coast highway. The girl got out of her convertible holding a dead owl in each hand like torches. She made the woman examine them and stroke their downy breasts before she spread their wings and wrapped their claws around large quartz crystals. The owl bodies she buried at the edge where the branches of the pepper tree extended so the living owls on the pole could preside over their dead. When the wings had dried, she removed them from the salt and pinned them to the ceiling above her bed and she hung the crystal claws in the window. It had not occurred to the woman that she would want her dead about her, that she, herself, would want to be buried here so that her heirs — and who might that ever be but the girl? — could caretake her grave.

By the time they had lived together for six months, the woman was used to the way things were. She had become used to the girl sleeping wherever she was, but she continued to track her, came upon the girl and Timber in tufts of dry lupine, the blue flowers long withered and replaced by small bean pods, wolf bean, that the woman never dared to taste, or hidden away among the thick stalks of fennel redolent with bees, or sleeping among drying clumps of tall mustard on the way to the knoll where the woman had planted two olive trees, or later in the dry, scratchy grey skeletons of sage and the yellow arrows of foxtails. She was used to conversations which started and never came to an end or ended and never resumed. Interruptions were like star bursts, queer, energetic eruptions that fell again like fountains of light.

One day, the woman awakened alarmed as if by a change in weather or climate. She went to the girl's trailer pretending her visit was casual. The girl invited her inside under the shadow of the wings of the owls tacked to the ceiling as if in flight. Pretending that she noticed nothing, the woman said, "This is paradise. Let's stay here forever. This is like the beginning of time."

The girl looked at her strangely. The woman felt the girl disappear. She was as startled by the abrupt silence as if by a sudden noise. As if Owl had swooped in through the open door looking for prey. She looked deeply at the girl who was there but wasn't there. There was something else in her place. Someone else. Another being entirely. When had it happened? Not in the moment. Certainly not. The woman flipped back through time as if turning the pages of the book of their life together, each day minutely different from the day before, a bit of each image fading, another image superimposed and darkening. She went backwards and came

forward again. Came to now; it was black as coal. The girl had been disappearing for a long time and the woman hadn't noticed or hadn't been
willing to acknowledge the changes. The girl had been sleeping under the
specter of the road kill and it had flown off with her.

It was unmistakable, how had she missed it?

"Don't be angry with yourself. It's not your fault. You just don't understand time or place yet," the girl grunted.

It was as if the girl had grown a hide that was thick and rubbery. There
were thousands of fine lines across her which deepened as the woman
watched the heavy body of the girl fill out, spread toward her ankles, her
legs disappearing, everything, arms, neck absorbed into gray, lined, heavy
weight. Mud. Now the girl was mud. She was heavier than mud. Mud balanced on bone, the specific gravity of mercury slowed down to a stand-
still.

"The rhinoceroses are dying," the girl grunted and when she raised
her head she was unable to hide the rough keratin horn for which she
might be killed. It was difficult to keep her balance with this grief-filled
beast overwhelming her. It was difficult to breathe. The woman had to
pull in her breath from so far away, from so long ago.

Against the flank of this huge animal, the woman was also forgetting
everything she knew. She could feel her mind filling with old gray spaces,
filling with yesterday and the day before and the day before, each day erasing today and falling like a mudslide, an avalanche of earth, stone trees, pu-
trefaction and petrifaction down into a dark pit of forgetting. There was
only this now. This first animal. This ancestor. The one who remembered
how it had been then. Before. Before what we call Now. Before. During
what we call Then. That was all there was to this beast. The ponderousness
of Then. How difficult it had been in the beginning. What it meant to
begin. The task of remembering. Of carrying all those centuries. Carrying the past now and carrying the entire future then. It made her bones
bend with the weight. It made movement difficult if not impossible. It
pushed today so far away it no longer existed.

This animal, the woman understood, lived her entire life in Then. The girl, who had said the woman didn't know how to understand time, was carrying Then, for herself, for the woman, for everyone, for everything. When she leaned up against the woman, the woman was overwhelmed with Then. She reached out her hand. She remembered being told there was a soft spot behind the rhino's ear. She reached for it and rubbed it kindly. The animal breathed a sigh of relief as Now reached to Then in this small and tender place. The hide was softer than she thought it would be looking at it. There were entry places. The rhino liked to be scratched gently, to be caressed.

"Put this burden down, little one," the woman whispered in the girl's ear, in what she thought might be the girl's ear.

"Someone has to carry it," she thought she heard the girl answer even if it was only a grunt. "And the rhinoceroses are dying out. Not dying out, really. Hunted out. The elephants too. They're so big and smart, you would think they could protect themselves."

"I really thought we were in paradise," the woman whispered.

"I know," the girl said with a voice laden with unbearable knowing.

"How did this happen?" the woman asked. The girl said nothing. The girl had once been so light and delicate. Like those small blue butterflies that close their wings and become a dry leaf and then open them to the light and shimmer like spruce sprouting. Now she was nothing like this. The blue she had been lost its light. It had become heavy, ponderous, dense as iron, ferrite blue, gray.

The woman stared into the girl's face and saw the changes occurring that she hadn't seen before. She was running the book backwards and then forward again swiftly. The last weeks passed in minutes and now the woman saw what she hadn't seen.

"Sit down and look at me," the woman said taking a stool and pulling it up to the small table that served as the girl's easel, writing desk, work surface and kitchen table. The girl sat down opposite, her arms folded defiantly.

No movement. No shape shifting. No white wolf. She was looking in the ragged face of a young girl who had been enduring unbearable suffering. Deep brown eyes stared out at her from the depths of human history.

And where had the woman been while all of this was happening to the girl? In bliss, thinking of Paradise.

"Paradise," the girl whispered as if imparting a great and dangerous secret, "never existed. It's not before, if it is anything at all, it's afterwards, and so no one we know, nor anyone that anyone has ever known, has known it. Certainly, you are smart enough to know that the Bible got it wrong."

"How do you know about the animals?" the woman asked.

The girl continued to stare at her.

"How do you know about the hunter?"

There was a long silence, equal to the first long silence that had introduced the girl to the woman and the woman to the girl. But there was no tree between them now. No trembling leaves, no shimmering play of dazzling light.

"Tell me," the woman said moving her hand gently forward toward the girl who flinched and moved back.

"Not on your life."

"It's not my life that's at stake."

"Well, how do you manage to live it so safe, Owl Woman?"

"The hunter? I forgot the hunter. Is that it?"

"You didn't need to remember. You have it easy. The hunter seems to belong to me. So I have to be like an elephant who never forgets."

"Are you angry with me?"

The slight movement of the girl's arm, fingers tightening into a fist which was just as quickly released. But the hand was no longer relaxed. Open fingers. Wrist slightly raised. Tension in the arm. A vein pulsing. It could become anything in an instant, a rod, a stick, a fist. However the woman would name it, it had become a weapon.

The girl began screaming again in the middle of her sleep as she had before. The woman would leap out of bed and run to the trailer. Sometimes she could awaken the girl and sometimes she couldn't. The girl would tell her nothing. She would go back to sleep and then she would scream again. Azul had once more taken to sleeping with her knife unsheathed in her hand and was awakening with cuts across her palm, dried blood. The hunter was back. "Nothing you could have done would have stopped him," she said but the woman knew that she was failing the girl.

"But these are dreams," the woman insisted. "I know how to work with dreams."

"How can you? You don't even know what dreams are."

It was not the first time the girl had maintained that she and the woman did not understand the world in the same way and so they did not live in the same world. In the woman's world, dreams were... well, anything and everything the woman thought they were. But in the girl's world, dreams were extra-dimensional events which overlapped with what people called reality or the day world. The woman had been trained to think of them as metaphors, as stories about something that was happening in the mind of the girl or in the everyday. In the woman's mind they were not little worlds of their own. They were not "real."

"You betcha they're real," the girl patiently explained.

"Can't you avoid entering them then?" the woman inquired earnestly.

"But why would I avoid my dreams? They're mine aren't they? They are part of my life, aren't they?"

She never saw the girl clearly the way she saw other people or herself. There were always thin layers, diaphanous films, shadows, mists, ghosts, spirits, sprites, entities, apparitions like the first vision of the white wolf treed by the woman's fear and misunderstanding, almost invisible ethers like the girl's stained glass of different colors and hues, translucent sheets of energy, whirling storms, winds, dust devils, cyclones, tornadoes, turbulence, all of which confirmed the girl's insistence that the world she inhabited was not three or even four dimensions but was layered with different realities through which she passed, or where she was hunted or where she did battle, or where she grieved, or where she hid, or where she lived.

"Can I go with you?"

"Don't you think it's hard enough without having to take care of you?" No matter what her state, the girl's laughter was irrepressible, it shot from her like a geyser, all force, sulfur and passion, and splashed down on everyone in its perimeter. "How would you manage when you don't even know there is anywhere to go and you're spending all your energy trying to get me to stay home? If you could tie me up, I think you would."

The girl paused and then added, "Timber comes along," only as if to reassure the woman.

"But..." the woman continued and then stopped with some alarm and shame.

Timber clearly knew what the woman didn't, couldn't know. Cognizant of the girl's continual peril, he was staying by her, bringing what strength and cunning he could across the lines that had separated human from canine for centuries. He had been getting old and now he was becoming an old grandfather alongside her, slowing in the hip, becoming infinitely tender. The woman knew that Timber was saving her life, but maybe he was also raising the girl the way only an old one can raise a girl, fearlessly and with resignation. He could teach her to growl, to bare teeth for the bite, to chew, to kill. And he could teach her how an animal dies.

Maybe his company assured her that his tribe had survived the proximity of humans, that he survived without a pack, that he carried the gene of freedom in his body and had passed it on to the wolves and mongrels who came from him, that it was in his fluids, the way freedom was innate to all waters, to everything that flowed, that his freedom could not be genetically altered even after centuries of domestication. But also, the woman understood that much as she hoped he would sustain the girl, his innate assurance was, whether he liked it or not, the assurance of the partially tamed and confined. The girl had started carrying something else, she was carrying the adamantly wild in the face of its enemies.

Not knowing what to do, the woman began coming into the trailer after the girl was asleep. If a wolf could guard her, so could she. She would sit on the floor, pillow behind her back, reading or thinking, watching the girl's frantic eye movements, the tension coming and going in the sleeping body, the labored and erratic breathing. The woman watched the girl sleep the alarmed heavy sleep of ponderous, endangered animals.

"Why?" she asked for the hundredth time.

"Someone has to carry it," the girl had said. "Someone has to carry it."

The woman could have said, "I will carry it." Azul would have roared, but she could have said it, the woman was thinking. The woman felt the undertow of quicksand and let herself go down and down and down to where the wretched girl was sinking.

The unbearable grief was everywhere, a deluge, a rainstorm fifty inches deep, thick slippery mud, caliche, the girl called it, that stuck to your boots so that you lifted a pot hole of it up with each step looking like the proverbial giant and unable to walk with any balance, teetering from side to side. Not any giant, not a fairy tale giant, the great beast's leg itself, the rhino's leg, or that of an elephant. An elephant in quicksand.

"How did this happen?" she was standing in the doorway of the girl's trailer, her hands on her hips, staring down at the girl curled up on her bed, exhausted from the weight she was carrying.

"You don't pay attention. You think it's all easy. You're used to getting what you want. You have to start at the beginning, but you don't know that. You think you can just start to fly whenever you want to fly."

"I don't know what you're talking about."

"I know. You don't know anything."

"What can I do to help?"

"Don't start on me. Don't ask me to tell you my dreams." At least anger enlivened the girl. She had risen up on her elbow, fury in her face like a charging animal protecting territory, hundreds of pounds hurtling through brush, sand flying everywhere. "What your friend, Mr. Friggin Siggy Wiggy didn't know about dreams could fill all the pits on the moon."

"What is it little one?" the woman was both confused and exasperated.

"And don't 'little one' me either," she exploded again. "Do I look like a little one? I don't think so."

There was the specter of a great beast, not shimmering like the white wolf, but a dark phantom, ancient and wrinkled, a grief-stricken hide, centuries old and equally heavy, a dismal smear of great weight that filled the entire trailer so that the woman couldn't breathe in its presence because it took up all the air with its sorrow. An anguish the woman didn't believe she could begin to approach.

All this caring she had done for the girl had only strengthened her sufficiently until the girl had the fortitude to go out and do battle. Like someone sending their kids off to war. Like the old witch fattening up Hansel so she could eat him. What a tasty dish I've made of my little one, she berated herself.

Meanwhile, as if the animals had not been enough, or because, somehow, the suffering in the human realm was a relief to her, Azul started painting portraits of people she had never met but read about. She painted the woman on the pavement who'd jumped from fifteen floors above. A man who had lost an arm to war. A man who had tried to stab himself to death. A blind woman who had been raped. A child who'd been locked in a basement room for twelve years. A woman whose twins had been tossed into a fire. She painted feet, hands, torsos, the back of their heads and finally their eyes staring out of black charred faces. When she finished these paintings which she named "Self Portraits: Children of Violence" after the novels by Doris Lessing, she locked them away in a storage space she had rented, the way one of Lessing's characters, the mad woman, had similarly locked herself away. On the door to the space, she painted block letters, "Don't Speak to the Inmates," and a yellow happy face which some undetectable sleight of hand rendered terrifying under the letters.

"Can you tell me anything," the woman asked the girl. "Can you tell me anything?"

"When you decide to take something on, you have to take it on from the beginning. You don't just get the end of it, the part you see and love, you get the whole thing, from the beginning, the whole package."

"Like you?"

"Well, you could start there. Like me. You want me, then you have to want all of me. Yesterday and last year and the year before. And the beginning."

"And..."

"And it's the same with the animals. You don't just get to have an obedient poodle with a diamond collar and a private trainer, you get .... I'm not your poodle or your unicorn or your magic white wolf. Oh forget it!"

"But you can't forget it, so you may as well tell me."

"Just figure it out yourself, Owl Woman, since you're so smart."

And then it was as if the girl had disappeared. She stopped speaking. She withdrew entirely into herself and whatever country that was. Now when the woman spoke to her, she looked at her blankly as if she didn't know who either of them was. She went to sleep and wouldn't wake up.

The woman called a friend, Clarice, as much for her name as for her assistance. "You can't wake her?" Clarice asked.

"She won't wake up," the woman asserted.

Together they carried the girl out of the trailer and brought her to her house, put her in the bathtub and sat beside her until she awakened under the demand of soap, scented oil and warm water. She looked at the woman with eyes that were still far away, puzzled, uncomprehending. "I have bad dreams," she whispered.

It was then that they began scrubbing the girl in the way of women performing *limpias*. They placed the girl on the stone slabs of the patio and attacked her with loufas, then they poured pails of warm water over her, washing away the piles of dead skin that accumulated under their diligent labor. On their knees, loufas in hand, they scrubbed and scrubbed, pouring pail upon pail of water on her until there were large heaps of dry skin, scales, hide, pelt, fur and the girl was smooth and brown, like the flesh of a tree underneath the bark, wood that was hand-sanded, smoothed, varnished, gleaming, They secured a heavy canvas tent on poles over a circle of stones, built a fire of pine logs — the temescal first described to the woman by the girl — and crawled into the shelter to awaken the girl's skin with steamy zapote leaves and eucalyptus branches.

It was an audacious act, violating all the principles the woman was so carefully following. It was the first autonomous, you could say autocratic act, the woman had made, as she put it to herself, on behalf of the girl. To protect the girl. "What are you protecting the girl from?" the woman asked herself. "From myself," she confessed. "And," she declared bravely, "I am protecting myself from this girl."

For it was certainly true that as the girl had become vulnerable to her, she had become vulnerable to the girl. She had seen that this was the girl's intent as they had carefully thinned the barrier between one and the other, and anything might cross over. In this case, when she was committed to protecting the girl from herself, the woman was also intent on taking back a part of herself she had allowed to slip without noticing it.

The heaviness did not belong to the girl. Heaviness was not intrinsic to the girl, it belonged to the woman. She had known this from the first moment she had seen the girl — the lightness of her in the tree and the heaviness of the woman below — but she hadn't known what it meant then, she hadn't known it was exactly the way things should and were to be. After they scoured her, as if with pumice stones, erasing all the fine lines which composed the map of age and time, after they sanded away the lines that were circumscribing her as if they had become a fine net that were dragging her back to Then, after they had expunged the prehistoric weight which had deformed her body, the girl was restored to the small animal she had always been.

The woman dug a hole in the wet dirt for the debris. It was a symbolic gesture and she was doing it for the sake of the girl and for their friend, Clarice, who would otherwise be alarmed. A matter of aesthetics. The woman knew the old hide wouldn't stay in the ground, wouldn't stay buried. She didn't know who would begin to paw at it. Timber? She doubted it. Coyotes? Would they come so close to the house? She was say-ing Coyote in her mind but she was thinking Hyena. If some animals could slip through the watery borders between one continent and another, why not all?

One way or another, the woman knew it was a temporary measure.

"That's the end of that," Clarice said, washing her hands more thor-oughly than seemed necessary. Then the three of them dressed and went out for dinner where the girl ate only vegetables, spinach, broccoli, car-rots, potatoes, as if she were grazing.

But, of course, it wasn't the end of anything at all.

It was only a matter of time, the woman was thinking as she observed the changes in the girl's disposition. Yes, she was alert again. The woman would have liked to say she was cheerful but she would have been lying. She was not asleep, she was not comatose, she was not in a trance, but she was not lively either. What alarmed the woman was the solution that girl seemed to have found to carrying the great tragic beasts: the girl had taken to painting them, to painting rhinoceroses. White ones and black ones. They had spears in them, darts, arrows, bullet holes. They were castrated. Where their horns had been were red gouges, wounds down to their gums. Then the girl set out to paint over the wounds, to heal the ravaged hide, to graft new horns upon the ulcerated sores, but the paint wouldn't stick.

Then she began painting the white Addax, an antelope the Italians had used for target practice during World War II until they were all gone. Also ant hills set on fire among heaps of skins, epidermis, cuticle, integu-ment. Dancing de-clawed bears jumping through hoops of fire. Mounds of tiger and lion skins, zebra hides, wolf pelts. Flayed animals. From time to time, the woman removed the drawings, smoothed them, hid them away. But they piled up again. Dead upon dead. The stink.

T he woman had spent the evening out and returned home after midnight on a moonless night. Coming up the long hill, the car headlights creating patterns on the foliage which was growing thickly to the very edge of the road, dipping down, tapping here and there against her windshield, she looked, as was her habit, for the light in Azul's trailer. In Norway people placed candles in their windows to mitigate the almost undiminished darkness which descended at the time of the winter solstice and Christmas. One walked through the dark wintry streets comforted by the small lights. Far less flamboyant than a Christmas tree, these chevrons of light had seemed to the woman to be extremely intimate gestures. "We are here. Greetings."

It was the same with the lights gleaming in the girl's trailer. "I am here." Professionally she would not admit it to herself, but the girl's presence relieved her of fear and anxiety. She was, she knew, security for the girl and the girl, in ways she didn't understand, also provided her with protection. Symbiosis of the best kind, she thought. We've become an eco-niche. Tree breathing out oxygen into the secret night, human and animal taking it in. Tree taking in the carbon dioxide the woman exuded. In and out. In and out. The cycle went round and round. She could feel herself yielding to the girl and the girl rising up in her, one creature becoming another, birth, death, compost and regeneration, light flaming and dimming, moon waxing and waning, light and dark waves rising and falling, endlessly. Yes, they would be together forever, she thought.

When she reached her own house, she was surprised to see lights on in the far rooms though the entryway was dark and the front window, the one she always latched, was open a crack as if closed carelessly, and all the blinds which she usually left open were drawn. The external lights which went on automatically, like an animal sensitive to heat and light, had been turned off. Walking back toward the trailer, she found herself looking for evidence of the girl. It was very silent. The door was latched and bolted from the outside. The combination lock had hung on the latch for months and the girl had never to the woman's knowledge used it. "Timber!" she called in a whisper. No Timber. "Azul!" No Azul. She tiptoed back to the front of the house. The girl's car was locked. She never locked it.

Fear. Unfamiliar fear. Not since the drug dealer had parked in front of her house had she been afraid of what might be inside or stalking about outside. No Timber, no Azul, no rustling in the leaves. No owls in the trees. No coyotes in the hills. No wind and no rain. An unnatural silence pervaded the land. As of something assaulted, injured and removed. She had never considered before the ominous presence of absence, the dark, not a thing unto itself, but the absence of light. The stars were shrouded by the clouds which until a moment ago had merely presaged rain. This is where she and the girl differed: she was admitting that she did not love to be outside. Whenever the girl was really afraid, she ran outside, threw herself on the mercy of earth and sky. But not the woman. Not in this moment. She wanted four walls, locks and telephones, the guaranteed safety of what was manufactured. Solid objects, joined, smoothed, sanded, varnished, sealed. These she felt would make her feel safe. She made her way nervously to the house. Whatever had happened to the girl and Timber, she would discover it from the inside out. She would make a telephone call. She would sound an alarm. Help would come. They would find and rescue the girl and her wolf companion. Everything would be okay. Azul would be restored to safety. The woman would make her a cup of chocolate. They would laugh about whatever it was that had come prowling and had momentarily frightened Azul. The woman would take measures to protect the girl better when she was away.

There was no reason to think yet that anything was wrong inside, yet she moved stealthily as if she were not approaching her own home which had been a sanctuary to her for so many years, for as long as she had lived anywhere in this lifetime. She reached out to turn the doorknob; it didn't turn. She had never locked the door in her life. Now she admitted it; she was afraid. She left the front door and went to the patio. Locked. She could not see anything through the windows. All the blinds were drawn. The back door. Locked as well. She tapped lightly on a window reasoning that the girl had been afraid and so she had locked the doors and now she had fallen asleep. Yes, certainly that is what had happened.

She didn't want to startle the girl so she tapped gently. Maybe she was sleeping in the front room, where it was dark. Yes, of course, she was there. And Timber was out somewhere in the hills. This sometimes happened. She returned to the front door and tried it again. Locked. She tapped gently on the glass panes. No response. She went to the side window and tried to see inside, tried to slide the window open. Impossible. As if a wooden rod was holding it in place. "Azul," she whispered, "wake up. Let me in." It was silent. Not the silence of an empty house, but the silence of someone who had stopped breathing. The silence of something withheld. The silence of refusal.

"Azul, let me in."

If there was someone inside who wanted her to stay outside, he was not making it known. There was no warning away. No sign of danger. If there was someone inside who wanted her inside, he had not set a trap, he had left no enticements. The door was locked that's all. An accident. Azul had been frightened by something in her trailer and come inside the woman's house and then, still afraid for some reason, she had locked the doors and then needing space and perspective, afraid of being cornered, she had gone out to one of her refuges in the hills, had taken Timber with her, and had accidentally locked the front door. It had slammed shut or she had, without thinking, closed the secured door behind her. She would be back soon. Then they would figure out how to get inside the house. Azul would know. She would find a way to jimmy open a window. In the meantime, the woman could sit outside in the garden and enjoy the night air. Or she could take a stroll, as Azul had, even if it were a dreary moonless night with rain in the air. The woman opened the car, lay her keys on the seat, took a sweater and began walking down the hill. Is this how it was done? Is this how one took a walk at night? She did not go into the fields even though she thought Azul was there. Somewhere. For the woman, a road was familiar. It had been made by someone. A path was different. Anything could have carved it out. Any animal, any vagrant, any force of nature.

She was about five hundred feet down the road when she heard the car door slam shut. She turned quickly and made her way back to the car. Whatever it was, she needed to face it. She was cold and tired and needed to use the bathroom and the temperature was sure to drop even further as it did every night beginning at midnight until 4 a.m. and she had else nothing to keep her warm until Azul returned. Everything looked the way it had before only the car was locked and the keys were ... she didn't know where the keys were. Perhaps they were inside the car or perhaps some-one, some thing, had taken them.

Whatever had gone after Azul was now after her. Shivers. As of some-thing alien entering her. She tried the door again and thought she heard something, something padded and heavy, sighing. The click of nails on a bare floor. An animal settling into himself. Timber. Timber? Unmistakably his sigh, a sweet curl of a growl circling down with him into comfort.

Azul?

Yes, unmistakable. The girl was in the room. At the window now, quiet enough, she could hear and smell the girl's breath. There was enough an-imal in her now for her to be able to detect human and wolf presences. A certain damp warmth coming toward her through the crack in the win-dow, an unmistakable spurt of musk, an animal aroused, watchful, ready. And the girl's scent as well, woody and fragrant but also tense. She could smell poise. She could smell ... hate.

"Open the door." And then when the silence settled like a heavy nox-ious vapor, she repeated the words.

She could do it, couldn't she? It would be easy. She just had to go to the car.... No, the car was locked. She would go the laundry room and get a hammer and break the glass and reach in and open the handle. She could do what she had always avoided by never locking the door. She could break the glass. Why not? It was her house. It would be easy to replace. Not a big deal. There by her quivering feet was half a brick she sometimes used to prop open the screen door. She picked it up and felt its weight in her hand, felt the clay like a dusty stain on her fingers. Tried tapping on the glass with it. "Azul," she called, "little one, wake up, open the door, I don't want to frighten you."

And so she took the brick and raised it and tapped the glass with it and covered her eyes with one hand and banged the glass with the other. Failing to crack it, she tried again, banging now more against what was in the house than against the glass, then more against her fear than anything else, against her fear of glass splinters, against her fear of the sound of crystalline shattering, against almost everything, against everything. The glass broke, the brick sped into the room, blood spattered and rushed down her fingers as, in a frenzy, she reached into the room, pushing the blinds aside, trying to find the door knob.

"Don't try to open the door," Azul said in voice unlike any voice the woman had ever heard. A voice that she knew from her own nightmares. A voice of gravel and stone, of rust, iron, the smell of friction, metal and acid. "Stand back from the door, bitch."

She did so. She heard the open window slam shut. Then leather footsteps crunching broken glass approaching the door. The blinds shifted a little. Footsteps again. A small light went on in the room. Stony faced, Azul was seated on a straight backed wooden chair facing the door. She had a long knife in one hand and a stick in another. A thick rope covered by slivers of broken glass was by her feet. And the leash that the woman had kept for the times she had to take Timber to the vet was tossed about the girl's shoulders but not attached to Timber who did not, as she expected, get up to greet her. He lay on the floor in back of the chair, not as if he was protecting Azul but as if he was sustaining her. The silent camaraderie between them was absolute, glass on the floor or not. Whatever it was she was thinking, he was behind her.

"Don't even consider trying to come in the house, Owl Woman. This is my house now. You stay outside. See what it's like, Owl Woman. Stop getting off on me. I'm not your fantasy. Get it? People live in houses. Animals live outside. You want to be an animal, Owl Woman? Make yourself at home where you belong.

"And don't think you're going to leave the hill and knock on some neighbor's door who will call the police or give you a nice warm bed and a shower and cup of tea and sympathy. Don't think you're going to escape me by finding someone who will cluck, cluck around you.

"Because I'll follow you and I'll hunt you down before you get anywhere and I'll tether you and you'll never get free.

"So you lie down right there, outside, where I can hear you whimper but don't you even think about howling."

She knew it now, the animal silence which was helpless before words. The animal fear which was helpless before will. The animal urge stymied by walls and doors. The hopeless, unrelieved animal hunger. The unappeasable animal thirst. The animal shame before humans. Retrained. Exposed. Visible. Observed.

"I have to ... pee," she squeezed out a voice that was certainly not her own.

"You mean you have to take a shit because certainly you can pee outside without any difficulty. Well, dig yourself a little hole, Owl Woman, with your fingernails. Use your silk pants or find yourself a leaf or use your hands."

" I ... can't...."

"Oh you will be surprised to see what you can do and what you can't. Sweet dreams, dear Owl Woman."

It was starting to rain. Maybe it was a warm rain, but it felt like glass slivers. The woman walked around and around the house and she could feel the girl following her on the inside. It was a kind of tether or it was a new kind of connection. A link. Chain link. A fence but not a fence. Something between them. Knowledge.

Yes, knowledge. She didn't know if she would survive it. She tried to think of what the girl might have done under such circumstances. There was that spot she had sat on before at the base of the girl's tree. Without the body of the girl to shield her, it was as exposed as any other spot. She had decisions to make: Wet dirt or wet bricks. Walking or lying down. Huddled or stretched out. Under a tree or directly in the rain. Covered with wet clothes or naked. Growling or silent. Sucking sweet and salty warm blood from her fingers or letting them scab. Opening her mouth to the rain or licking the water from the leaves. She thought of getting under the car but she didn't. Cringing or agreeable. She decided on attempting dignity.

It was the middle of the night when the woman dragged herself out from under the tree and went out to the back yard and began digging up the old skin that she and Clarice had scraped off the girl. By now it had mixed with the dirt but there was enough there for the woman to run the particles through her cut fingers reviewing the words she had been thinking the night they had stripped the girl of her hide.

The heaviness doesn't belong to the girl, she had thought then. It's mine, she had thought. It belongs to me. But she hadn't taken it in, she had buried it.

She began digging. It was not raining as much as it had and the earth was only wet at the surface. Not digging really, but scraping at the soil with her fingernails and then with a stone and then, deliberately, with her fingers and nails again, not fearing that her nails would break but hoping, illogically, they would be strengthened by black earth packing underneath them, thinking of the hard yellow curve of Timber's claws. Deeper down it was dry. It took a long time and she had to pass through the deep blue twilight called the Hour of the Wolf before she came to the skin shavings, tiny translucent scales which had come from the girl's body. The sequins had turned silver in the reflected light from the window and the lightening sky as she gathered them and laid them out, as she had once seen moons of minuscule silver fish drying into crescents alongside a lake in central Mexico. She did what she would never imagine she should, could, conceive of doing, she returned these fish to the rain water which had gathered in an empty jar and seeing them sparkling there, she drank them down.

It was different seated under the tree with icy pale light whitening the sky. The woman felt truth swelling in her like an infection, red, hot, pulsing, spreading through her system along geo-historical lines. Like a drone, the thought repeated itself in her mind, the heaviness was never supposed to be in the girl, it was to have been in the woman. She was the one to become heavy with elephants, rhinoceroses, hippopotamuses. Because she was older, she could carry more of the weight of it all. Rhinos first. They ran through her, but they did not stay. They were followed by hippopotamuses, crocodiles, a series of rumbles, booms and great claps of thunder. And then, as if they had been waiting for her all along, the elephants arrived in torrential herds. The earth shaking, her own body pulsing with them. She couldn't tell if they were running in her or she was running with them, in them. Whichever it was, she gave herself away to them. It was like a swoon and she did not resist. It called to her and she went down. Into them. Dissolution.

She was in this state of mind both trampled and mesmerized when she heard the almost silent movements of another animal and sensed, without hearing or seeing, Timber in the vicinity. It was not pity for the woman, she knew, but Timber's need that caused the girl to open the door and let the Wolf out. Instantly, she became alert as any animal would to the presence of another mammal and followed him with eyes and ears and mind as she had never done, aware of signs that had in the past been invisible to her. His routine, for she noticed it was a routine that had always seemed random and haphazard to her, appeared organized and purposive. She could almost smell what led him here and not there, the presence, no, not necessarily, also the absence of scent, something to be overlaid with his musk as well as something to be freshly marked. She always let go of her own bodily fluids with far less consciousness, reading a magazine on the toilet, nothing that would occupy her, so as not to waste time on the body, thinking a piss was a piss, a shit was a shit. But he, clearly, was thoughtful about the act and preoccupied with far more than a physical release and a flush. There was an intelligence here she had never recognized and a round of concerns she couldn't begin to imagine. No surprise, then, when he raised his leg exactly over the spot where she herself had pissed and had not, as he did now, scratched dirt over the slow seeping puddle.

She was explaining his behavior to herself in ways that were familiar from research, always ending up at some version that projected a need for protection or innate aggression. Or he was covering for her, didn't want other animals, coyotes or cougars, to sense a wounded or lost human because it might draw them onto this territory. He didn't want any other scents but his around; his scent meant: Don't cross this boundary. In the past, she would have been embarrassed to anthropomorphize in this manner, to glorify what she had been taught was pure instinct. But in this moment even such explanations seemed shallow before other possibilities, ones, she was thinking from a part of her mind she had never known was there, that humans might not even consider. For example, she was thinking that he might be participating in a ceremonial rite which only another animal would understand. Hadn't she seen him walking along with some of the female dogs who were also allowed freedom and afterwards lifting his leg on the spot where the female had just hunkered down? This was the thought in her mind as Timber, having wandered out of her purview, returned and stood above, licking her face and hands. He would have licked more of her if she hadn't gently pushed him away and he growled a sound she had always interpreted as satisfaction, but now she thought of as resignation as he settled down. He placed his back against her, shuffling and arranging himself, not, she was thinking, for his comfort but to indicate to the one who had never bothered to learn his language that she might, she, too, might lay down with her back against him. Once she got it, she acquiesced and then stretched full out flat on the damp ground with her face on his neck and her arm about him.

For half an hour perhaps. Then this didn't seem right either, woman and wolf under a tree that Azul had claimed as her guard tower. She lifted herself heavily and began trudging down the hill across the invisible path where the madman had driven wildly before getting out of his van. She made her way across the wild oats and foxtails, down the narrow path that animals and humans had cut through common use round the thicket of oaks, skirting the poison oak and tramping along scratchy walls of thick brush, not knowing where she was going or what she might be looking for, until she came to what could be considered a decent bower in the chaparral and crawled in among the vines and spindly trunks, careful of the briars, and settled in, telling herself the fib that this bed of decaying leaves and twigs would serve her well. When she was settled, Timber nudged at her calves with his nose to give himself room and laid himself down alongside her so that her legs were fully aligned with his body and relatively warm.

When she awakened, the girl was standing above her, assessing her without any sign of remorse or worry. The sun was up and Timber was gone. Not a bright day, a dimly lit day, light crusting on her like the mud that was drying on her arms and face.

"You'll want a bath, Tecolote" Azul said. "You're bloody and your clothes are a mess."

"A shower will do. It doesn't matter." She paused as much to see if the night had erased her ability to speak or whether she was simply hesitating to return to whom she had been just a few hours ago. "How did you find me?"

"Timber. I didn't know I was following him but he went ahead when I started looking around."

The girl turned on her heel so the woman would not be embarrassed as she crawled stiffly out of the underbrush, not knowing if the girl, who was expert at making dens and nests, had found the woman's choice enterprising or not. It wasn't only that she wasn't practiced at living outdoors, she was older than she would admit and the sleep had not refreshed her. Only after they came to the front door did the girl speak again:

"Watch out for the broken glass. I couldn't get it all up."

"A vacuum cleaner will take care of it. And a glazier."

"I can do it. I'll make you a stained glass window, if you don't mind waiting for a few days."

"It doesn't matter, does it, Azul?"

"No, it doesn't matter, but you do need a hot bath, Doña Tia Tecolote."

S he showered and put her clothes in the laundry. She picked up all the glass and cleaned up the house which the girl had trashed. In a few days, the girl replaced several panes of glass with stained glass versions of a procession of animals marching toward a sun at the top of the door. How the girl had managed to capture longing in glass, the woman did not understand.

It was as if the solstice had come and gone, as if they had passed through the darkening of the light and were involved in the coming forth by day. But not so simple, the woman knew, wary of her own insistent optimism and her tendency to read omens in her favor. And if changes were to take place in the girl, they had to occur in the woman first.

It had all started out of love for the girl and then, later, out of a sense of duty. She would have expected it to go the other way, but her love had not been sufficient or the pull of responsibility was greater. What had begun as a spontaneous gesture which, in her best moments she knew was kind, if chancy, and in her worst moments she labeled as overreaching and romantic. How could she have thought she could take the girl in and continue with her life as it was? Why did she think she had more of a chance to help the girl than Carmela and Dusty had had? Didn't she trust they had also wanted to heal the girl? She hadn't seen who they were any more than she had really seen the girl. Why not simply accept the fact that she had had no choice but to take the girl in and in doing so she had bitten off more than she could chew? What had she been thinking when she called the girl down from the tree, and in whose interest had it been? What was it she had thought she loved in the girl and what was it she had been determined to heal? These were questions that the woman needed to ponder.

What she had loved and continued to love in the girl was the animal.

What she had loved and continued to love in the girl was the animal that she believed the girl loved, valued, was trying to protect. And she had not — no! she had been impeccable, hadn't she? — she had not tried to exhume the animal from the sacred ground of the girl. Nor had she ever imagined fixing the girl. What she loved and wanted to protect were states of being that seemed to unnerve and threaten others, or that the girl hid from almost everyone, except on occasion the woman, or so it had seemed. What she also loved and what she also felt responsible to protect was a certain elusive and intangible fluttering between different states of being, a course as cunning and rapid as the flight of the red throated hummingbird or the streaks of fire emerging as the aurora borealis.

When she was around the girl, that aura was never far from the woman's awareness, whether she perceived it as shimmering and translucent or resonant as the odor of blood. It was the very essence of the girl and it contradicted everything the woman had thought she knew about the nature and possibilities of her own life.

The woman couldn't presume that she had been transformed. That all it took was getting out of the house and sleeping where she fell down. She didn't presume it could occur through will or her calculated decision to take on the burdens that were inappropriate for a girl exquisitely designed to protect small things. But, nevertheless, she was determined.

It wasn't the end of the battle, the woman kept reminding herself, it wasn't only a matter of removing the girl from the fray, and bringing her to safety. It was, if the woman were to become trustworthy, the beginning of something she had never really considered taking on, though she had spoken eloquently to herself about just such a possibility. A battle continued in the vicinity of the girl and someone had to confront it. Someone who had not to this moment even imagined the battle or that it might belong to her. She was someone who had looked at such — what would one call them? — spirit wars? — with disdain. Struggles in domains she had not deigned to take seriously, therefore struggles she herself had most cleverly managed to avoid, struggles which, in the past, she had entered only to extricate others. Now, she realized, this struggle was hers. She enlisted.

She picked up her weapons.

For the next few nights the girl slept without being awakened by nightmares, even if the woman did not.

The woman began dreaming of the savanna. In the beginning, she was amused, as if the dream world were a cartoon. She noticed that the great white hunter who had been stalking the girl across the savannas had been temporarily waylaid. His Nissan had broken an axle, he couldn't string it together with wire. He was being forced to spend the night watching his back. But she also dreamed that he was planning his next move.

These were unlike any dreams she had ever had before. They were both less and more real than she considered possible. She began to entertain the ideas the girl had presented to her: dreams were real and represented travels in other realms equally real — whatever that meant. These were the words that came to her. They made sense but also she didn't fully understand them. Sometimes, she looked at the girl hoping she would explicate it all for her. But the girl said nothing except that she seemed carefree. And so the woman kept her own silence.

One night she wandered more deeply into the dream than she had before. She was not dreaming of the savanna, she was on the savanna. It was as if she heard the girl whispering caution in her ear: "Everything you do now, Owl Woman, will affect this world we both live in. Don't be naïve, Owl Woman. There is no absolute line, distinction between the worlds."

"Where am I?" the woman asked. The woman heard a gasp as of the in breath of a startled impala and the presence of the girl dissolved.

There in the distance was the Great White Hunter spending the night under the thorn tree, a strange place to hide because he would not want to climb it if a threat came in his direction. But he would not be there long. He had several guns, a great deal of money, both on him and in bank accounts, many bank accounts, associates, if not friends, and a certain puissance that could dominate situations, as disagreeable as he was. She caught his face in her binoculars just as the moon rose so that she could study him before she went on to wherever she was being led. He was the kind that had colonized the area for decades, hunting animals to bring them back to his ranch for breeding so that their offspring could be hunted there at his convenience or for his profit. He vacationed by hunting chimps, killing the mother to get the baby to sell as a pet or for animal experimentation; the drug companies paid well for this illegal booty. A poacher working for foreigners. An adventurer wanting a few hide throw rugs for his whorehouses. A scavenger searching for the keratin horns of rhinoceroses. There was no telling the origins of the hunter. His face changed, he tanned, darkened or lightened, browned, blackened, yellowed, whitened, his eyes folded, unfolded, lengthened, rounded, browned, blued, grayed, greened under his pith helmet, his bush hat, his khakis, his desert boots. A shapeshifter of a different order. No, not, not a shapeshifter. The shape wasn't changing, no variation of essence, only a change of mask. It was the way power worked. It was consolidated here and then it moved there, like money over a stock market which was the same money here or there, accomplished the same ends, or like a highly tuned racing engine set now on this chassis or another, but the same engine, the same game. The girl had alluded to the particular chemical scent of domination which followed the hunter who was tracking her, but she had never quite said this was no ordinary man: this man was a sorcerer.

Ivory. He was after ivory. The woman understood this instantly. Despite or because of international agreements, because of quotas and black markets, because of government storehouses of confiscated contraband, ivory which could not be sold legally, ivory became an even more precious commodity and he was after it. He was after the forbidden in the righteous manner of a free man protecting the rights of free men. This was his modus operandi. Now that she knew this, and hated him for it, he would be after her. She had succeeded in turning the hunter's attention from the girl to herself.

The woman studied him through her high powered binoculars as if he were a specimen. Fascinated. She liked having him there within her sight, distance dissolved, so vulnerable, so available. She didn't know how long she watched him before she understood something which made her shiver.

As long as she was watching the man, he had her. He had caught her. She was fixed in her observation of him. She was in his dream. He knew where she was. She had to be near enough to him to see him. He knew she wouldn't go away because she was protecting the girl, and so he would find her as soon as he was mobile. It was only in one dream that he had broken an axle and couldn't fix it. In the next dream, he had solved the problem. He had all the time in the world. He was as powerful in this dream world as he was in the day world. The realization struck her in her heart. She had a choice, a slim one, which might mean her freedom. She could try to remove her attention from the man, she could move her concern and concentration elsewhere, leaving him under the tree with the car battery running down. She could try to get out of his dream and enter her own. But that didn't work either. He was under a tree, pouring a gin and tonic. He reached into the cooler for ice. He had repaired his car. As long as she was who she was, she was pulled into meeting him on his own terms. That was her training. She wouldn't, couldn't, let him go. She had to come up with another strategy.

She needed to make an alliance with something else, an alliance that would transform her permanently and remove her from this dimension in which he had her pinned. In order to do this, a change of mind was required. Even in her dream, she felt vertigo the way she had when she had first given herself to the girl. But she held firm and in moments she was with a herd of elephants and a voice inside her said, "These are your people." She didn't know what this meant but she felt it in a muddy body.

Whatever the woman did during the day, she found herself among the elephants most nights. It always began the same way. She'd be driving along the savanna and this time, her car would break down. Fear would arise in her and she would find herself disintegrating from the force of it. She would force herself to leave the car and begin walking away from the road. Some instinct arose in her, familiar because she had dreamed it before, but otherwise foreign, to leave the known world, that danger lay there, that the car breaking down was a gift. She never remembered the exact details of what she had dreamed the night before while she was dreaming, but was nevertheless sustained by inner knowing that this was exactly what she needed to do, that she had done it before, or others she loved had done it before, that the road had been the wrong road from the beginning and she was supposed to go through the grasses in the direction of the trees at the foot of the far hills. Once she went back, put the key in the ignition, turned on the engine, revved it up once, twice, let it idle. Left it running, until it emptied and died and the sands covered it.

Or she took a train and something possessed her to jump off when they were nowhere before he could flag down the train and board. Or the one engine plane she was on crashed and she walked away from the wreckage. One important thing: walk away.

It was hot, dry, dusty. The wind displayed itself in ghostly yellow swirls. She would walk, it seemed, for hours. She found a pole that someone had abandoned that she used as a walking stick. Could she protect herself against him with it? She doubted it but it was pleasant to lean on it as she plodded on. After a while, she wasn't walking on flat land but following a slight incline toward banks of tall pale green grasses obscuring a stream. Movement in the grasses. It could be lions, but she persisted in believing the elephants would protect her the way she had seen one protect an elephant calf.

Elephants had been by the river and a young lion was stalking them from a ridge. A mamma elephant was browsing casually in the grasses, her young one, only a few inches behind her, head tucked almost under her tail. The lion was coming closer, hunkering down, skulking through the underbrush until he was directly behind the elephants, poised to spring. Was he already in midair when the woman saw a flash as the mother elephant turned and flapped her ears once, throwing the lion back unsteadily onto his haunches so that he staggered before he slunk away? A stroke of her trunk across the little one's head and back, a gentle stroke, reassuring, affectionate, and she was engaged once again in the grasses, the little one nuzzling just a bit closer to her teats and the other elephants only seemingly oblivious, but rather most definitely, ardently alert.

The woman would come upon the elephants more quickly than she expected. From a distance, she didn't see them. She would feel lost or frightened and then she would be among them, afraid of leading him to them and afraid of being alone. She found herself within the wall of them, cloistered within their citadels; ramparts of gray flesh surrounding her. Then a door opened, not only a door of flesh, but a door somewhere, in the country to which, without realizing it, she had been applying for a visa for her entire life.

One of the elephants separated herself from the herd and came toward her. It was the old one, the old grandmother, the ancient one, the one the others followed. The old one lowered her head enough so that her great eye with its tough, wiry eyelashes was gazing directly at her. Then it closed. And opened again. Between the opening and the closing and the opening again, something transpired.

The woman was infused with an enormous grief that knew no bounds. It was exuded by the elephant but it was also as if the great beast was drawing it up from the center of the earth, from an ancient burial ground, from a grave site of elephant bones. A deep lament as if from a tusk hollowed to make a horn to be blown at the moment of death.

Then she saw that she had come to an animal ritual. The elephants parted, opening yet another door, and she was brought to the perimeter from which she could see a dead bull elephant, his tusks amputated, stretched out on the ground. They walked around and around in a circle and she walked with them. The slow pounding of their feet on the earth as they walked created a rhythm which entered her body. It didn't pass through her, it sat in her. Her heart slowed to it, tuned to it, as did all her other organs. They began to function according to this rhythm. It made her heavy. But it had much beauty to it. The beauty of a tuba. Of a bass. Of a bass clarinet. Of a bass fiddle. Drum beauty. And every now and then the air was punctured with a subsonic wail of misery and anger.

She didn't know how many days she walked among them in her dreams, treading that gray circle. The bull's body relaxed. The jackals gathered in the distance. His flesh softened and the weight of the bones pulled him open as if he began to liquefy. She could smell him and his odor entered into her too. Sight, scent, rhythm was filling her. She forgot her human body and her human thoughts.

She began to know other things, things she couldn't repeat to herself in English or any other human language. But she knew them nevertheless. She had known them forever. They came from Forever. From Then. And when she fully understood these, other knowledge proceeded from Then through Now. She breathed it all in. The current grief was a shock, a concussion of thunder followed by acid rain. It was everything she had feared. She began to dissolve in it. She needed something to protect her. Not something to dispel it, nor a rain slicker to protect her from it, but something to help her withstand it. Bones large enough to hold it. A thick hide. A different time zone. A larger context. A longer and more appropriate history.

She began to incorporate all of this. On the surface, she appeared the same, a small woman among a herd of elephants. She was barely taller than the grandmother's leg. But on the inside, she was increasingly as old as the grandmother, as large, almost as full of understanding. She knew that by the way she was walking, by the ease with which she followed the rhythm, by the blessing of the heaviness inside of her.

When she came to a boundary where the grasses yielded to tangled bush, thorn trees and thick shrubs, the grandmother approached her and ran the edge of her trunk down the woman's hair and along her torso. It was a caress of exquisite gentleness. And then the woman knew that the grandmother had loved the bull. That they had been lovers. She saw the grandmother walk out of the circle, she watched the sensuality of her stride, the long, sinuous, graceful movements, slow and deliberate. There was a perfume in the air, an erotic mist, a silver sweat that shimmered on the grandmother's back. The grandmother strode back and forth, gathering trunks full of leaves and then bundles of grasses and went out again and returned and then went out again. She took mud from the bank of the thin stream and packed the holes where the tusks had been and spread the leaves and grasses as if they were pale pink petals scattered over the body of her beloved.

These dreams had became her real life. She dwelled in them when she was awake and tried to live her life accordingly. One night, she went to sleep very early. She lay on her back as if unwilling to sleep and also ready to fall asleep immediately. When she entered the savannah, she waited for dusk and drove cautiously, raising no dust. It was as it always was in her recurring dreams. She saw the hunter in the distance, preparing himself for his quest. She pulled to the side of the road and got out of the car, hiding behind the open door.

For days, she had rehearsed this sequence, again and again, until she was certain it would work, even to the point of getting a permit, learning to shoot, buying a shotgun with mounted optics, reduced recoil, a Remington 870, and practicing at the range. "Deer or turkey?" the gun shop owner had asked her, leering. "Deer," she said, wanting to wink, but afraid of where she was being taken.

When she was skilled enough, she took the shotgun she had kept hidden in the trunk of her car back to the shop and sold it back. "Scare you?" the man had asked.

"Not my thing, it seems. My boyfriend sure is disappointed."

She moved without moving. She took the shotgun, steadied it on the window she had raised to exactly the right height, aimed through the sites, and shot. The woman had never killed anyone before.

She did not go to the elephants that night. She did not want to bring harm into their vicinity and refused to protect herself. Willing the girl to stay asleep, she remained alert until dawn came, a flare of radiation against dead trees, brilliant enough. From the metal thermos that had always resembled a weapon to her, she poured water over her hands. "Stay dead," she muttered, slid into the driver's seat, turned the key, started the engine and drove toward awakening.

All the rules were changing as were her thoughts and perceptions. She began to construct a life in accordance with what occurred to her in the dreams and doing so, realized that this had started much earlier, that she had been coming to this for all the months she and the girl had been together.

When she had first met the girl, she had claimed the girl had been taking all her attention but now she knew that over time the girl had taken her over the edge. Accordingly, she had been losing interest in what had previously mattered so very much. It was not that she was falling into dishabille so much as she was ripping to shreds the usual garments of her days and life, finding everything she knew in a state of tatters, her knees and elbows naked, bending eagerly, as it were, for bare ground. That's what she wanted — bare ground. Barefoot on bare ground. She did nothing. She wanted to do nothing. She had always thought that anyone in such a state of mind would be distracted, entranced, withdrawn. She had associated undress and shabbiness with depression and as a clinician it had alarmed her. But to the contrary she found that she was extremely alert and very keenly engaged and exceedingly curious about patterns she had never noticed before. The flight of birds, for example, or the ways in which water flowed along the banks or over rocks. Movements and counter-movements that resembled music more than anything else. She pondered the intervals where one seemed to convert to another and sometimes she was unaware of whether she was seeing or hearing. The call and response of the owls or the ways in which the coyotes' shrill exaltations reverberated across the mountains gathering moon-white speed like a flood or avalanche rushing down. Or she watched overtures of small birds fleeing down pinnacles of clouds at sunset followed by the dark movements and timpani of crows.

The local paper featured an article on bobcats declining because of rat poison. She had never talked to her neighbors before; she went on a short-lived rampage and searched every cabinet for anything that might do harm. From a distance, the girl seemed amused by her domestic zeal, but said nothing, though it seemed there was a bounce in her gait, or the din of keys was louder.

All day long, the woman meticulously unfastened her mind from what it had become accustomed to, from ideas and theories and beliefs. It was a small and satisfying labor similar to one to which she had once devoted several weeks of the summer when she had painstakingly removed all the dead leaves, twigs and branches from an ivy that had wound over and over itself across a white stone wall. It had been so thickly entangled, one year's growth weaving itself under or upon another, that the wall had become invisible and the vine had seemed a dormant solid mass of green. But then slowly as she extracted first this and then that narrow brittle limb, that tiny shoot, that bough, lifting out the weight of it to allow clusters of dead leaves to fall to the ground, the white wall made its appearance and upon it a complex and spacious circuitry of brown lines and leafy greens. So much dead weight gone.

Now that the debris of her assumptions and beliefs had been as studiously removed, she saw a fine network of relationships and could eavesdrop on the subtlest of conversations between creatures she had assumed were only circumstantially related. Blinded by what she had assumed were instinct and habit, happenstance and indifference, she had missed the entire world of involvement and interchange. And here came old Timber Wolf nudging her to follow him as he surveyed his territory and repaired the boundary lines.

She awakened slowly from these ventures across the borders and walked heavily to the bathroom, slightly disoriented by the bowls of white porcelain, the cold tiles, the rolls, sheets, carpets of plastic, vinyl, acrylic. Everything she still did as a human was surprising her. That she could still walk upright, that she had hands, that she needed to write things down, that no one but herself knew about the gray, wrinkled body of love and grief inside her.

The world she knew was changing completely. She stopped everything she had done for a lifetime to eliminate or cover up scents, body odors, smells and began to read the aromas as carefully as she had once read print. She could smell rain coming and night falling, shifts in ozone, leaves opening to bird songs, the perfume of an opening flower, honey on the bee, the scented insect calls across the miles and the flight path of a bird hanging in the air like a vapor trail. Animals walking across the field lingered even after they were gone. Scat told her who had passed by and when. The air was alive with messages and imprints. Buzzing. She didn't know if this was sensation, sensory perception or memory which was developing in her.

It was not easy. Janus-faced, she found herself dividing, a gulf developing between the two faces facing in opposite directions as if the very corpus callosum of existence had disappeared.

She had a day life in North America and a night life elsewhere. She studied sound like an acoustic engineer and within a short time she could differentiate some of the seed syllables of Timber's speech and though she couldn't answer him in his own language in any comprehensive way he understood, she was able to differentiate certain basic elements of his communication. This was more than she had ever attempted before when she assumed he should understand her.

She spent her waking hours listening in order to reconstruct the universe. And at night she fell into another world altogether. The sound beneath sound, the ultraviolet, the infrared of sound. Subsonic sound. High pitches that shattered her thinking even to imagine and low rumbles that reconstituted her very bones. It was this latter that brought her once again, full circle to the elephants.

S he began to study elephants in the daytime. Above all, their mourning ceremonies intrigued her. Her dreams were not only dreams. That is, they were not fabrications of an awakened imagination. Elephants did engage in ritual behavior particularly around death. Everything the woman dreamed, was confirmed in something she read. The untimely, unnatural death of an elephant at the hand of a human drove the members of the herd into paroxysms of rage. An elephant bent upon avenging the death of a loved one was formidable indeed. The elephant never forgot the offending party and never made a mistake. She could be on a vendetta but she remained precise and patient. She or he could wait for years. The guilty party was never safe if he was anywhere in the area of the injured elephant. An angry or grief stricken elephant did not always act alone. Communication between elephants, she learned, is exceedingly complex, takes place over long distances, over many miles, across night fears and dream time.

She came across a peculiar story and she could not shake it. At a local zoo, a bull elephant, the head of the herd had gone berserk. Not knowing what to do, the zookeepers separated him from the herd, but he was uncontrollable and finally they shot and killed him. The entire herd was maddened. The animals were confined in safe quarters, off limits to the public for a long time. Time did not heal the situation. Finally, under pressure, the zoo contacted an animal communicator who, it was claimed, might be able to intervene. When the unimposing, scrawny, bony woman, whom no one would have tagged as formidable, came to the zoo, she insisted that she be allowed to enter the elephant compound, alone and unarmed. She could not and would not do the work otherwise. The officials having already failed twice to deal with contentious animals and being afraid of failing again by challenging an unimposing female, relented, but not before they drew up the necessary papers disclaiming any responsibility. Then, according to her implicit instructions, they removed the iron leg chains which, whenever humans were present, affixed each animal to the wall. The woman entered the compound.

In one of the large doors of the barn-like structure which was the holding tank for the elephants was a smaller door which she opened and passed through and closed behind her. After several hours she emerged. Did she seem even more diminutive or had she taken on the size and presence of the elephants? She demanded the elephant bull's head, which had been preserved for scientific purposes. Even with the head, she refused all help but insisted it be placed on an electric cart which she would drive into the compound herself. It could not be done outside; the elephants had the right to their own private council. She went back into the compound with the head.

We can only imagine what occurred. Perhaps the matriarch and the youngest bull lifted the head with their trunks and placed it gently and respectfully in the center of their circle and then the animals and the communicator, circled it swaying, grieving throughout the night. Late in the next day, the communicator emerged to announce that the elephants were calm. "We mourned together," she said, "and now they are reconciled to his death. You will bury the head; you may not use it for research."

Something was finally happening inside the woman. She was becoming simply other or other to herself. There were others inside of her. She had never been pregnant and now she was full of seeds exploding out of her like dandelions subordinating gold into gray and bursting open. Until this moment there hadn't been any other reality within her; she had thought she was a singular world, a world without elephants. But now that was all changed. There was an elephant inside of her, a herd of elephants or the woman was also an elephant. An elephant without a fence around her. An elephant outside a zoo or a circus. An elephant without a chain around her ankles. An elephant on her own recognizance. Free and independent like Timber Wolf. A wolf and an elephant hanging out together. In the way

Hindus allowed the Holy Cows to wander through the streets. This elephant was beginning to think for the woman. Elephant wisdom. The woman felt old. Ancient. She felt a history within her that came from prehistory. A vision entirely outside of language. If the woman could, she would have trumpeted.

Here was a question: Was the woman sometimes the woman and sometimes an owl and sometimes an elephant — which one of these smoky beings was she? Was this a protean situation? Or was she all these creatures at once, or did she become one or another at random or in sequence? Was this shapeshifting or multiple personalities that she was engaged in? Watching the girl these past months, the woman had been thinking about internal communities as models of health. Now she was worried that she was going mad. She didn't have any answers, but she was getting a headache.

"Don't let yourself reduce real life to pathology," Azul warned as she strutted into the house without knocking, her steps firm in work boots, her keys dangling from a metal fastener attached to her belt by a chain. Everything jangling at once, keys, fastener, knife, chain.

"Don't start reading my mind again."

"I don't read your mind. It's too much like trashy literature. These days it's full of great drama."

"I thought you liked great drama, Azul."

"Only when I live it. In books, it's not convincing."

"A few days," the woman said. "I'm going to stay out on the land for a few days, I don't know how long. When I come back, we'll see."

"We'll see what?" Azul asked, her face puckering into a monkey stare as it did when she was confused.

"I don't know, now, but I think we'll know then."

How easy it was to accomplish what she had always thought was impossible. The words having been said, the deed followed effortlessly. She took the tent she had bought when she had imagined the two of them would go camping but had put back in the laundry room. She took a sleeping bag and mat, she took lots of water, a journal, matches and a flashlight. She took some dry fruit, nuts, cheese and crackers, bird seed for the birds, dog biscuits for Timber, should he join her, and some candles in windproof holders. She took toilet tissue, a hand shovel and a jacket. Even this seemed a great deal although it was far less than she had ever imagined she would need.

"Aren't you going to tell me…?"

The woman did not let Azul finish the sentence. "No, I am not going to tell you where I will be. If I don't return, it won't matter where I was and if I do return you won't have needed to know."

"You don't make sense anymore."

"Don't worry. I am as sane as I have ever been."

Azul smiled as both knew this was and was not intended to be reassuring. The woman was not concerned about the girl.

She knew the girl would be fine. The only thing she needed to think about was herself and that as little as possible. And, as they say in myths, she set out.

Avoiding where she had slept the night she had been locked out, careful not to leave a trail as she didn't want to be tracked or found, having become skillful in the dreaming, she hiked a long distance into the park, crisscrossing her own trail, taking paths that anyone would assume were too difficult for her, stopping, resting, drinking water, starting up again, she came upon a rock face with a small cave that seemed not to have been used by people recently. No smell of human urine. There were no beer cans or metal tabs. There was no sign of recent fires. No plastic bags. No scat. Outside, there was a level area shaded by trees.

She settled in to the cave warily after she was certain there were no snakes and that bats didn't inhabit it. She took her things out and arranged them and then she put them back in her back pack. She was afraid and she didn't know what to do. She scattered bird seed outside in a circle by the trees but not too close to the cave. To defend herself in a cave, she would have to be powerful, fierce. Tree security did not require strength. She considered which trees she might climb. It was ridiculous. What was she afraid of? A few blue jays came and several squirrels. The quail clicked and called in the distance but would be too shy to approach until they became accustomed to her presence. She took out her journal. She meditated on what the first words would be. After an hour, she wrote, I AM HERE in block letters in the center of the first page. An hour later, she added the date.

She sat inside, then she went outside, then she came in again. Repeatedly and restlessly. She had thought she would know what to do and how to be from having watched the girl with such focus and intensity, but soon she recognized she was the one here, and she was here alone, she had not been alone on this land before and she had to figure everything out herself.

She drew a larger circle under the trees so that she could sit inside it. She put down white corn meal and bird seed. It would have to be sufficient.

In the cave, she found herself ruminating on what she needed to let go. Outside, she tried to imagine what was needed for a new life. In other languages and mind-sets, months earlier, she could have identified the two states of mind as divestment and acquisition, or sacrifice and self-realization, but these ways of thinking didn't serve her. Because she wanted words, couldn't be without them, she finally settled on the dynamic her Buddhist practice described as emptiness and form. That made her suck in her breath and then she laughed. The sun had set. It was a warm night.

It was getting dark. She did not want to use a flashlight and she couldn't make a fire; this was fire country and fire season. She scooted against the dank back wall of the cave and hoped she would sleep. Across the hills, the rolling calls and yips of the coyotes. It was different being here and listening to the one she and the girl called the Singer, who, the woman believed, led the pack with her strong alto voice. The pack came closer and the woman astonished herself. Rather than stay in the cave, she came outside, snuggled into her sleeping bag, she leaned against an oak. She wanted to be with the stars, the animals and the night. Little creatures she couldn't see came and scratched at the seeds she had scattered. By now, she should have been hungry. She wasn't and knew she would not eat for the time she was here. Finally, she slept. It was a good beginning.

In the days that followed, she tried wandering about as she thought an animal might peruse its territory and then returned to her camp and stayed there learning to see what she had never seen before. For the first few days, she wrote down everything: comments on her own life, regrets and insights, attempts to understand the girl, ruminations on the therapeutic process, its possibilities and limitations, her fear of the great animals that had come to her, and the dreams, and her concern that she couldn't always distinguish them from the daily life. These reveries yielded to other kinds of observations: the camaraderie between deer, the coming and going of birds, the earnest life of insects, but then she stopped and simply sat, walked or slept. The words she felt she had needed in the beginning left her for a silence neither reflective nor hopeful.

Even as Timber avoided or forgot her, for he did not make an appearance, the great beasts, after a time, left her to herself, withdrawing to the shadows they had inhabited before she met the girl. Dimly, she understood that if she was to come to them, be with them, she would have to start out on her own, from a place called beginning deep in the center of herself. Her own journey increasingly confirmed, not the girl's. And so, finally the girl fell away from her too, became a dim memory, someone who had come to her at the right time, a psychopomp of sorts, utterly unexpected and unrecognized as a guide, who had sent her off or back to the proverbial fork in the road where she had stepped in one direction but could have stepped onto another path, perhaps the one she was taking now.

She thought she was returning to a moment when she had made a primordial choice, but perhaps it had never happened. As a child, she had lived outdoors. She had been a great walker and more than anything else preferred to walk to the ocean and observe the waves. Yes, she had lived outside. She had walked day and night, even in the rain. And then one day, she seemed to prefer a house. It was if she had come inside and locked the door. As a child she had been fascinated by ants. She left them trails of crumbs and tracks of sugar in the garden on the lawn, in the cracks in the sidewalks and the teeny grassy niches between the cement squares of the driveways. She watched them for hours, especially intrigued when the small black creatures, mouths full of pearly eggs, paraded past her in a line. One day, without realizing she had made a shift, she laid down lines of borax so that they would disappear from her sink and table. Maybe she didn't remember the first ant she had squished between her fingers, but she remembered one she had, and the divide that occurred as she took its life.

The last night she was there, she was awakened by a chilling cry. Cougars, she had been told, sound like a mother wailing, and this was such a cry. All the possibilities ran through her mind. She could return home. She could crawl into the cave and light a fire there. She could offer herself up as a holy sacrifice or as a gesture of reparation. She could stay where she was, her back up against the tree trunk, still as the many small and invisible creatures about her, observing the natural course of events and her own responses. That is what she did. She leaned against the tree and stayed alert through the night.

She entertained no ideas that the cougar could or would read her mind, recognize her goodness and leave her alone. She had no thoughts of communicating with this creature. She had no thoughts whatsoever. She was a being that wanted to stay alive and the cougar was a creature who wanted to stay alive. No matter how much the girl suffered, she still wanted to stay alive. And the great elephant matriarch who had seen the mutilated body of her partner, she also continued to want to live. That was the equality between all of them. By the end of the night, the woman was no longer afraid. She was ready to take care of the girl, not because the girl was injured, fragile, or disturbed, but because she was a girl, and the woman intended to assume the responsibilities that were hers as an adult that the girl had been carrying until then.

In the morning, when she packed up her things and made her way back home, she came across three small chewed bones, as if deliberately aligned, preposterous as that seemed, on the path. Vertebrae of deer, fresh blood on them, a little gristle. She picked one up and put it in her pocket and left the other two exactly where they were.

"How was it?" Azul asked.

"It was thoroughly unremarkable," the woman answered as she was unpacking her backpack.

Azul queried her with an intense glance. "You didn't eat?"

"No."

"But all the bird seed is gone."

"Yes." She was placing a small plastic bag stuffed with toilet tissue in the garbage.

"Clean or soiled?" Azul asked, without trying to hide her amusement.

"Soiled."

"You brought them back? You're very civilized."

"I have a reputation to keep up, it seems."

Azul was seated at the table. She had taken off her boots and was running her feet over the curved lion paws which formed the base, massaging her instep against the polished wood again and again.

"I want to tell you something about elephants," Azul said.

The woman was poised. "I thought you didn't know anything about elephants."

"I know what I know."

"I was reading a newspaper article which claimed that the adult elephants are teaching the younger elephants to hate humans. The adult elephants are so upset about the raids on their territory, about zoos, circuses and poaching that they are actually transmitting their fury to the younger elephants who grow up hating humans as if it is as natural as breathing. I read that the elephants are being culled in order to keep their numbers down.

"What does culled mean, Tecolote?"

"It means that they are being hunted and some of them are then relocated." Before she finished the sentence she knew she was lying. Lying to protect the girl was lying. It was worse than lying; it was violence.

"It means that they are hunted and killed. The matriarchs first. The bulls. Sometimes all of them. Sometimes the young bulls and cow are relocated."

"Why don't they say what they mean."

"People are trying to create a balance so that there aren't too many elephants for the territory and so they don't wreck the land where the people live."

"You mean the people settle into the elephant's land first, and then they decide if there's enough room left for elephants. You mean they are hunting down the elephants."

"What I mean is that sometimes instead of shooting and killing all the elephants from helicopters, some of them are being moved to other places where there are fewer elephants. They are relocated."

"And?" Anger. You couldn't say the girl was angry, you could only say there was anger where the girl was. "What are you telling me?"

"That they move the young elephants. Young bulls. Not yet mated. The teenagers, I guess."

"And?"

"And they go mad. They never forget the slaughter. They become rogue elephants. They don't have family anymore, a culture, a village. They don't know anything. No one is there to teach them anything. No one to take them in hand. No one to show them how things are done. No one to show them the water holes, the migration routes, where the food will be, the way things were and ought to be."

"So what do they do, Owl Woman?"

"I don't know, Azul."

"They hate. That's what they do." Azul said. "I think hate is the only thing they have. When you only have one thing, it better be a gun. But you don't agree, Owl Woman. You don't think that. That's what I think. You think if you only have one thing, it better be love."

"I don't know what I think. Do you want to fight about it?"

"Oh, no. I wouldn't fight with you. It would be unfair. You wouldn't win even if we were arm wrestling and you got to use both your arms. I have to be so careful around you. I could really hurt you."

"Do you want to fight?"

"No. Forget it. I could lose myself and hurt you."

"I'm not as innocent as you think. I know a few things too about how things are."

"Well, maybe. But even if you were once street smart that was a long time ago. And you've gotten soft."

It was clearly not a good idea to argue with Azul at this moment.

"I'll take it on, Azul. You don't have to worry about it."

"You'll take it on?" Azul could not have spoken with more derision. "You? You'll take it on?"

"Yes, I'll take it on."

And then, she dared. "I know something about this. I know something now." There it was; she was crying in front of the girl. She had said what needed to be said; she had told the truth.

"Sit down, Azul, and have something to drink, relax, because I have already taken it on." There it was.

"I'll also make us dinner," she continued.

"Like what?"

"Like barbecued chicken."

"Barbecued chicken? I don't think so, Owl Woman, unless you catch it first in your talons."

"What would you like then?"

"I'll go to the store." She paused to respond to the woman's unspoken words. "Yes, I fucking well can drive." She softened. "And yes, I do have money.

"We're not going to have meat, Owl Woman. Is that okay? Can you stand it?"

"I rarely eat meat anymore, you know that."

"Rarely is too much. Can you stand not having meat?"

"I can stand it, Azul."

"Are you sure? Can you stand behind this, Owl Woman?"

"I can stand behind it, in front of it, on it and in it, Azul. What about you?"

"I want some cokes and I'll get you wine, Tecolote. And then I'll cook, okay?"

"It's a deal."

"Do you want some money?"

"I have the change from last time. It's enough." She was smiling. "You set the table outside and I'll shop and cook. Ceviche, okay? Rice and beans. Have you ever been to San Blas? I was born in San Blas and learned to prepare ceviche there."

"You weren't."

"Doesn't matter. We'll turn the garden into San Blas. Look, the fog is coming in. In a moment it will wind itself completely into the vines of the jungle."

A change in one person cannot take place without a change in another. This was becoming most obvious though the woman marveled that she had never realized this before. Once again, but now, finally, because of what the woman had done, no, because of what the woman had taken on, no, because of what the woman was allowing herself to become, the girl was also different than she had been. A system of shapeshifting. Something enacted here with consequences over there but without direct causality. No billiard ball hitting another billiard ball. Nothing like that. An eddy in the air that passed through them and seemingly altered them but without noticeable impact, a radiant wave passing through one and then the other, molding each as it went by. They were sharing a common life so one became something else in the proximity of the other. A see-saw. As one came down, she raised the other up.

If the woman was heavy inside, but grievously, joyously heavy, she was gladdened to know what she was coming to know, learning to walk so, to be sure-footed, so fervent in her new, in a new but true, she thought, true nature. How to say it? That is, how to think of it? She was relieved, greatly relieved, to have taken on the heaviness, the concomitant afflictions, the dangers, the laments of the old ones and then, most happy when she saw the girl was lightening. Was comfortable and easy in her flickering, now one being, now another.

The woman wasn't thinking about her as a girl anymore. Not a boy either. Not quite a hybrid. Not a man nor a woman, not a mongrel of gender or culture, not Mexican, nor Chicana, nor Peruvian nor Colombian, not Maya, Cuna, Arucanian nor Patagonian, not human only, nor only wolf, not monkey, not coyote, not bird, not one creature or another, not spirit alone but an earthly and unearthly assemblage of different elements in joyous and unpredictable exchange.

Everything seemed to be back to the way it had been when the girl was in the tree, when the woman had first glimpsed — had first glimpsed what? — had first witnessed spark and glimmer, flash and transformation.

The woman wanted the girl to be free, to live as she wished, among others, or almost altogether outside of human contact, to choose in each moment to respond to this world or the other. Azul's appearances and disappearances were like particles taken up into one dimension then spit back or out into another. She was here and then she wasn't, whether according to will or without willingness, no matter. Did she simply sometimes sneak away into the high mustard, passing through thin stems with dainty leaves, flounced with tiny, pungent yellow smears of flowers that crowded against each other, parting for her, as she nibbled — taste exploding the way yellow does when it burns the tongue — that closed afterwards so no trail or sign of a trail was left? Or did she disappear into another language, being rendered invisible or absent?

It had not happened often that the woman's hopes had been realized, but as soon as the woman began accepting the weight of her dreams, the girl began to rejuvenate.

If the woman had been naïve before, she was no longer naïve since the dreaming. She didn't expect the hunter to resurrect, nor did she think that the forest rangers or poachers would track her down to take revenge. But she knew there were other hunters and poachers and she had not saved the world or the animals. Her ambition had been to protect the girl, to take it on, as she had promised herself she would and as she had told the girl she had, and as long as she gave herself to the dreaming, despite her trepidations and night sweats, she had been, it seemed, successful.

The girl was beginning to emerge as from a tree carved by an invisible craftsman; what had been, her past, falling away as so many wood shavings. First Azul said, she was no longer interested in large mammals. Then, when the woman showed Azul the portfolio of her earlier drawings, Azul said, it wasn't her art work, that it wasn't her style. Later, Azul smiled indulgently at the woman's interest in elephants. Finally she repeated that she, herself, had never had a single thought about rhinos, elephants or other African mammals, not in her entire life. She said, these animals must belong to the woman, that for herself, she preferred the songs of small birds.

Azul immersed herself in silence as if it were a pool of holy water. Then she began making sounds the woman had never heard before. Each sound worked on the girl as if she were clay and it was creating a shape for itself out of her body. ooOOhoo she was mourning dove and her body fluttered. wha AAA HAA she was quail, a sharp parabola of sound and the whir of wings. A series of screeches, high pitched calls and bamboo rumbles turned her into jays, hawks, and crows. It was when the girl uttered her music composed of harmonies of dove and quail, she was beyond anything the woman could understand because she could not yet follow the girl, might never be able to follow the girl into the domain of the trill. Human language worked its own magic on people, but this was a change of another order altogether. It wasn't merely a linguistic feat, mastering the sounds, the whistles and calls, it wasn't mere versatility of lip, tongue and breath, nor the gift of a good ear, nor diligence, it was a kind of swoon that one had to enter, the slipping off of a skin or hide, the raw offering of oneself up to the other that was demanded if one were indeed to hear rather than listen, to speak rather than imitate.

These sounds were altering Azul or, as the girl might say it, if she would say anything about it at all, she had become the sounds themselves. The woman hadn't known that if one fell into language, it would change one, that the very words one used created a world which entered into one's pores like a mist penetrating the leaves of trees. Afterwards one was distinctly different because the desert bloomed and riparian niches flooded and dried out and each became something other than what it had been a moment before. The girl was and was not ever who she was or wasn't or had been or would be. Each creature gave its words to her and she took them on and she became them and uttered them as her own words, thereby making sacred covenants with the creatures and living among them in their own worlds.

The woman knew that the girl finally trusted her because she let her see this.

So, it follows, that according to the see-saw, or the dance, or mutual arising causality, the net of all beings, call it what you will, the girl was altered by being freed from what others saw when they looked upon her, while the woman was changed because of what her gaze fell upon. What she was willing to see. What she saw when she was no longer walking, as most people walked, by looking at themselves in a mirror. No wonder they stumbled and fell. She had so long ago, it seemed to her now, taken on the labor of picking them up, brushing off their clothes, healing their wounds and consoling them without having any idea that what they really needed was to learn how to walk in the world with their eyes wide open. Well, how would she have known that if with all her training experience, she had, herself, never been taught how to walk with her eyes open, looking about her at everything other, everything that was not herself.

Now, heavy with the old knowledge, having come upon it before the final cull, and so prepared to be informed by this lightning bug, this firefly of a girl, the woman actually began to see what she had never been able to perceive before. Some creature in the grass who otherwise would have been invisible. Lizard. Snake. Deer. Coyote. And then a white wolf in the distance. Mustangs, far, far away running through the hills. Bear in the distant mountains, beyond even the azure of peaks, thousands of miles north. Eagle, also far north and Condor to the south, beyond her vision but in it nevertheless. Past and future and so the girl was not ever far away because beyond was suddenly close at hand. Laughing. It was not fear or strategy that was changing her from one being to another, it was pure exuberance, pure joy, pure grief.

Released from the tyranny of time, place and expectation, Azul began painting wolves. She did a sequence of wolves beginning with white pups born in the moon-scented arctic night, the pack glimmering under the sheen of stars, the shining tumble of one wolf upon another, the frosty hunt and the feast of ivory bones, everything so milky and silver except for the droplets of red, accents of birth blood, dawn, tongue, bloody gristle, and ending with the calm death of an old wolf, like an old grandmother who had volunteered to go out on the ice after her teeth were worn down, ruby-eyed in the setting sun on the tundra.

After completing the canvas where the old wolf fed the black feathered scavengers, Azul came home with Frio. Frio was three months old. Pure white. An Arctic wolf probably without any Malamute in her at all though the sale of a purebred was illegal. "89% Arctic wolf," the breeder had said with a wink. The wolf pup had been born near an artificial lake in the desert. It was not wolf territory any more than the semi-arid mountains that the woman and Azul inhabited, but there were trees on their land to shelter Frio against the summer sun. Frio was the first of the litter, the alpha female and had, the breeders said, been born on Azul's birthday though the woman thought this, too, was a ruse executed through a sleight of hand after Azul had shown her driver's license for identification purposes. She was the first cub that Azul had picked up and she didn't put her down again, not even to write a check. Azul knew that she would never fence Frio though she described the fifty square foot chain link pen, twelve feet high, she had prepared. An exquisite artist and draftsman, she enthralled the breeders with the drawings she created on the spot, and who would doubt her after that? With equal finesse, she signed the legal papers agreeing to all the restrictions, attesting to the exact cautions and conditions she would observe when raising the animal so it would do no harm to humans and left, Frio in her arms.

She drove home with Frio in her lap and set her down in the woman's garden where the white wolf cub might have hidden forever among the densely packed shrubbery, flowers and rose thorns, if Timber had not appeared. But the cub, seeing the old wolf, was no longer afraid, never again, not of anything, not even when Timber growled or snapped at her indomitable frisky nature.

As long as Frio was small enough, the girl kept the animal on her body, tucked into the crook of her neck or under her arm; she slept naked with the wolf on her chest, sucking on the girl's nipples for all the woman knew, or nestling into her ribs. Waking, she cuddled the wolf under her blouse, or brought Frio out from under her chemise, blouse and sweatshirt, jaggedly torn open at the neck so the animal could breathe, to place her in the woman's hands, cooing appreciatively as the woman took the pup gently and placed Frio against her older, softer breasts.

"Comadre." The girl was pleased. A week later, she was carrying Frio in a sling that she attached either front or back as she walked. At first she never put her down, but then she brought the cub more and more frequently to the woman who was carefully instructed how to care for her as godmothers and grandmothers frequently are.

How quickly Frio grew. She was not to be long in the girl's arms. In no time at all she was following Timber into secluded places where he taught her to hunt the creatures small as she had once been, birds, squirrels, lizards, field mice and there were bloody offerings on the bed and carpet in the girl's trailer and on the worn threshold of the woman's house.

They were an unruly pack. Sometimes Azul or Timber searched out solitude, but by the evening, they gathered and tumbled about each other, passing morsels of food from one mouth to another, or fighting each other — snap, nip, snarl — for a bite of chicken or a sliver of bacon. Azul became as carnivorous as the other two and wanted nothing to do with the carefully prepared vegetarian foods she had favored.

Old, wise and protective grandfather wolf was to go through yet another transformation as he became the uncle, a necessary unit of the wolf family. Not every wolf couple breeds each year. One couple parents a litter and the other wolves become aunt and uncle cub sitters. Timber had been completely disinterested in the black and white mongrel's mongrel puppies even if they had his genes. But he felt responsible for Frio, reigned her in when she was too rambunctious, grabbed her by the neck or the muzzle when she wandered away from the territory he had circumscribed for her, and nuzzled with her when she wanted to rest within his paws. Over time the puppy was fully integrated into the household except that Timber would not allow Frio to get between him and Azul when he decided to lay by her side. And then, it sometimes seemed to the woman, that he deliberately brought the puppy into her house and left Frio there, and searched Azul out and lay down with her, his sleek and hairy back nestled into her belly and her arms around him and her face in his neck.

This is not the end of the story though it could be if stories followed story rather than life. Here we have it all, the woman thought. Myself, Azul, Timber, and Frio. A holy family of sorts. A quaternity, dare she think, of reconciliation and hope. Paradise. The wolf lying down with the lamb; for wasn't the girl a lamb, wasn't she the woman's little lamb?

"Sentimentality doesn't suit you," Azul rebuked the woman who was staring teary-eyed at Azul as she stroked Frio standing sleek, yellow-eyed and long legged, an apparition of grace, the muse herself, the incarnation of the mysterious white wolf of Azul's paintings and dreams.

What a fuss to make about getting another pet. The woman could involve herself with such inner babbling and save herself from the descent implicit in acknowledging herself as mother or godmother to a wolf. But, but, which one was the wolf that she was taking on as kin? Or to put it another way — which broke her heart to ask — did any one of them, could, would any one of them belong to her?

The law of nature. Frio was a great beauty and Timber, even in his old age was powerful. And how could she resist him? Or he her? The woman didn't know when they became lovers or what Azul thought of it. It happened, as such things do, outside the human realm, without the tedium of discussion or negotiation. The girl was sleeping in her trailer or out on the hills and who knew where? And Timber and Frio were out in the hills, and who knew where?

When the woman saw Frio and Timber together in the field the way she had seen Timber and Azul sleep together, her heart broke. It was so unexpected a vision that it unhinged her and a door of sorrow opened wide. It was not the first time she had seen this but it was the first time that the two of them were together without Azul and without the woman sharing their animal warmth. She came upon them as she might have come upon a secret, the two curled into each other as lovers nestle everywhere. They both raised their heads slightly, saw who it was, and settled back into sleep with a sigh. Timber's snout deep in the soft down of Frio' neck, the fur parting slightly from his breath. The woman sat down by them, they stretched their legs slightly and then relaxed as she stroked first one head and then the other. Kindness exuded from them with each breath. Timber had forgiven her. That was the thought in the woman's mind: "Timber has forgiven me."

Timber Wolf was old. "Poor Old Timber Wolf" the woman had cooed to him before Azul had come. Poor old Timber wolf had once had a mate, Loba. She had been his first love. They had been together three years. It had been before the woman had moved to the land, before she had known anything she now was coming close to knowing. It was before she had thought of being an animal. Before she had met the girl.

The woman had lived in a house in the suburbs and she had had two wolves, Timber Wolf and Loba. Two wolves in a small yard in a house in the suburbs. Loba was the wild card. The woman hated living where she was living but circumstances insisted upon it. Loba did not understand these circumstances. Loba wanted out. When the door opened, she would escape no matter how careful the woman had been. Loba had been a force of nature and nothing contained her.

Once Loba had broken through the back fence and pounced on a small poodle with pink ribbons walking dutifully by her mistress' heel, the pink leather leash hanging limply between the woman's arm and the dog's pink rhinestone collar. She had the poodle by the throat when the woman got to her and though she was afraid, managed to pry Loba's jaws open.

Once Loba jumped the fence, opened the gate and she and Timber took off. Two days later, the woman received a call from Animal Control. The two wolves had found a rabbit hutch some twenty miles away. Cornered and muzzled they were being held in detention. Loba was quite calm when they took her out of the back yard but once she was in a cage she was ferocious. The woman suggested they put Timber into her cage with her as he was not only calm, by nature, but a calming influence. The man at the other end of the phone merely snickered and told her she had a few hours before the wolf would be dead. "Come get the bitch or we're putting her to sleep."

Now that she was remembering, the woman was remembering everything that she hadn't remembered when Timber had insisted himself upon the neighbor's dog. Loba had been in heat and she had tried to keep Loba in and Timber out of the house but Timber had come in the window, leaping the five feet from the ground to the sill, breaking the glass, mating with Loba among the shards.

Unable to control anything, the woman had given Loba away. A logical solution. Now that she saw Frio literally in Timber's arms, she understood the cruelty of what she had done. The cruelty of innocence. Or ignorance. Which was it? Had she known what she was doing and refused to let herself know?

"If we find this wolf free again," the Animal Control people had said, "we will kill her, pups or no pups, before we call you."

She had not known what to do until she had met a man who trained animals for the movies. Synchronicity, the woman thought, as if it were always benevolent. She had assumed that an animal trainer loved animals. Then she had assumed that agreements made between species were honored even though she had broken such an agreement.

This is what she had to acknowledge: the animal trainer had made his way into her heart. He had taken her through his little zoo but had not called it a zoo. She, accordingly, had not thought of how the animals were confined even when she saw the large cage with a cover on it. She had wanted to know what was in there. "A cougar," he had said. "She's in her time. She's in estrus," he said with such utter tenderness that she had found herself yielding to him even before he asked.

"She's quite out of her mind. But when I talk to her quietly and put the blanket on her cage, she quiets down. Sometimes I come back at night when everyone has left and I sing to her."

How could a woman resist such a man? How could a woman not think this was the place for a wolf and the progeny formed in her the night of windows breaking and broken glass? Oh, the man had been kind and merciful with his hands upon and within her own lonely and bloody body and had awakened early and had, as they had previously agreed in the dark, taken the wolf as if for a walk.

She had never seen Loba or the man again. The man had said that Loba was going to live on a local ranch, that she would run free, that the woman and Timber could visit her. Then the man wouldn't answer the phone. Loba, the secretary said, was in Texas or was it Wyoming? No, it was Alaska. Yes, Loba was definitely, certainly, without a doubt fine. Wherever she was. The secretary was certain. The woman began to watch animal movies obsessively, looking at each wolf litter, at each wolf, looking for her own.

She had given Loba away, taken a lover for herself, immediately finding a place to live on the edge of the wild where she soon discovered she didn't have to build a compound for Timber. "A fence 12 feet high is the law in Pennsylvania and we're working on getting the same law here," the Animal Control people had said. Maybe this territory would have satisfied Loba's need for territory. Maybe the woman had been completely wrong when she had assumed that Timber would and Loba wouldn't respect boundaries.

Without thinking, the woman had given Loba away, without asking what it would mean to separate her from Timber, without ever considering that Loba might have also loved the woman and would be bereft without the two of them.

Had she given Timber to Azul or Azul to Timber as an act of contrition? Timber had accommodated to the woman. He had become her companion. He had eased her loneliness. They lived together seamlessly. Then the girl had come in Timber's old age. The woman had lived alone with Timber for ten years. She had said, "Timber is my mate." Then the girl had come. The woman had given them to each other or they had found each other, and the woman had acquiesced.

Now the woman understood the gesture that the girl had made. She had not gotten Frio for herself. She had followed her dream of a white wolf, but it was not for herself. She was, herself, the white wolf she had dreamed. The girl had made a gift to someone who had saved her life. She had found Frio and had brought her home the moment she, the girl, was able to sleep alone. She had known that Timber did not love her so much as he loved and protected the wolf in her. First he had invited the girl and then he had allowed Frio to sleep between his paws. From this bounty, he offered the woman forgiveness.

usty and Carmela telephoned from time to time to check on the girl and all four had fallen into the easy habits of neighbors. When they were going on vacation they asked the woman if she would check on their house. She parked her car out of sight and entered the house, checked the rooms, watered the plants, turned on the sprinklers. Waited. Turned them off. Everything was as it should be. Such peacefulness. After awhile the woman roused herself from her sweet reverie.

Something was to be done before she went back home. She was alert to the fact of it, but she had no idea what was to be done. So she began to circle the grounds and found herself at the sycamore where she had first come to know the girl. It had been so long since she had been here. She circled again and again. She stopped, and then she circled the grounds again, and circled the tree, counter-clockwise so that she could descend, as the girl had assured her was necessary to beginnings. Round and round but not to her own beginnings — they were irrelevant to the way now though they had been central to her life and her profession — but to the origin of her real life that had begun exactly here. Turning and turning, abandoning thoughts, words in the velocity of the spin until, afraid she would disappear herself entirely, she sat down hard at the base of the tree and looked up.

Where was the girl? She couldn't see the girl among the leaves.

But she saw something. Just the way it had been. A shadow. An apparition of white. She felt something, some imperceptible trembling. It was exactly the way it had been. Irresistible. Where was the girl? She had to find ... her ... It ... whatever was up there. The woman stood up. She was going to have to learn how to climb a tree. She had no ladder and refused to go into the house for one. She had no rope but refused to look for any as well. She had nothing but herself which was more, she felt, than she had had in a long time.

After a few attempts, she knew that she had to remove her shoes and then she realized her jeans were an impediment, that she might have more friction by wrapping her bare thighs around the trunk and scraping her way up than attempting the same shimmy up with the cloth sliding between. She hid her shoes and jeans and, as an afterthought, took off her blue blouse and placed all behind the jade plants which formed a border between the women's property and the neighbor's, wondering what it meant to undress in the easement, to leave her clothes in the no man's land between the two houses. If there had been a tree in no man's land, she would have climbed it first and then made her way across to the sycamore as a way of claiming no man's land for the others, for all the non-human creatures.

It wasn't true, of course, the free zone called no man's land wasn't outside the law but rather belonged fully to the law, was claimed by power and media companies, electricity, television, telephone, etc. No man's land belonged to man; that was the truth of it. Still the phrase gave her a boost. And the boost got her up the tree.

And here she was where the girl had been, exactly, she remembered, as the girl had been. From this vantage point, she tried to visualize herself there, below, then, when the magic of the girl had exuded from the branches in a smoke of pale first blossoms while she, the woman, had sat beneath the tree stodgy, inert, stubborn, stable, certain and so uncertain at the same time. She had been thinking then that she had understood the girl, when it was obvious she couldn't have understood anything the way she understood it now. Now that she was in the crook where the girl had sat. Now that she was here in this domain. Now that she had come here. Now that she understood that the tree was a destination and not a hideout. The tree was the local equivalent of the mountain that one climbed in order to ask the essential questions about the meaning of life.

The woman squinted and looked up to the halo of white that was forming and reforming itself into shimmering mercy.

"Loba," she said, "I've come to kneel at your feet. I've come to ask for a pardon," as she humbled herself before the kindly, expanding white paws of light.

Everything became diaphanous. You could call it a meltdown.

Meltdown was not the word she would have chosen, though she had selected it. It was rather other than that. A reduction of dearly held ideas and perceptions rendered into a soup of syllables, phonemes and letters from which she would have to construct a new language appropriate to the reality of the creatures who spoke it. A fragile and most delicate composition of sounds she had never made before in her life but which were exiting from her mouth in an ecstasy of hope toward the brilliant light that was taking form, that the branches were arching up to meet and to hold, and that could not, she saw, be other than the one, the one she had not recognized in the past, but now recognized, the one who was manifesting, who was displaying herself, who was willing to be seen, the one, the great god Loba herself. Call it a howl. A first attempt at howling.

That spirits walk on the earth in the form of animals, this was not a new or unique idea. Various peoples had thought it, continued to believe it, since the beginning of human life, for over a million years. That a particular animal might be not only a spirit in animal form but the spirit itself. That an animal itself might be divine, not only the mask of the divine. People had believed that as well. Pan, for example, the goat god. Or Leviathan.

Also that animals often sacrificed themselves for the sake of human beings, had a prior sacrificial arrangement with the species for reasons unknown to the woman. That animals came and offered themselves up instead of the person, or in order to teach them something or to transfer their power or manna to the human. As if their lives meant less or were most deeply served through such a transaction. Or that humans were less advanced, spiritually, if, regrettably more advanced technologically, than animals, than anything else really, and so everything was in the service of human development so as to reduce the impact and harm of human activity. Loba, for example, who it might be said had sacrificed herself, had been sacrificed, so the woman could have Timber as her consort and everything that had come from that.

But what if the idea of animal sacrifice for the sake of the human was a delusion and an atrocity? What if it was not always appropriate to kill, martyr or sacrifice the god? What if the god had needed to be preserved rather than destroyed? What then?

She had come to talk this over with the God herself in the very place where she had first seen Her without understanding anything of what she saw at all. She had come to shed a bit of her human arrogance with the ease and certainty, the unease and uncertainty, with which she had taken off her shoes, socks, jeans, blouse, underpants and bra. She wanted to be naked in front of Loba the way she thought it was essential — from some point in one's life on, the sooner the better — to be naked before God. Loba had also been a white wolf; the woman had forgotten that entirely.

Yes, it had certainly been a different vantage point that the girl had had from this place in the tree. She had seen more rather than less than the woman had seen. Now that the woman could see more, she was relinquishing her understanding of how others might see her if they knew she was up here. Instinctively, and so without checking her balance, she peered down to where she had once been looking up. Of course, she lost her balance and scurried to right herself. A fall was inevitable, as the girl would have warned her had she been there. Fear went through the woman like a wave just the way she had seen it happen to the girl, similarly shattering her. Then, as there was no place for fear to settle, it hovered about her like a veil of fog but without, as the woman knew too well, covering her though it did obscure her vision.

When she righted herself, she realized it didn't matter. This is what she had not understood. The fear turned out to be immaterial and disappeared the moment she changed her posture and returned to herself. Fear was a frequency from elsewhere without substance where the woman was presently ensconced. The girl had not been the first to try to explain something so essentially inexplicable to the woman who had listened with reverent and insufficient understanding.

The woman placed her awareness in the body she had once occupied there at the base of the tree, a body ensorcelled with a dream of its own benevolence, a body rhapsodic with its own courage and generosity. She saw that the body, then, didn't have the capacity to understand what she, the woman, was doing now, indulgent as the body might have been; the body was banefully unappreciative of the woman's activity except as an expression of terror or madness. The girl had been right. The woman had had a social worker's mentality and she would bring it to her own current behavior given half a chance. It was clear that the woman had to separate herself from any ideas she might have had once about who she was now. Such concern was distracting and potentially dangerous to her well-being, but more importantly, to her spiritual development. The woman she had been had withdrawn in order for this new woman to develop and she was determined not to resurrect the past and destroy the present. She refused. She would not.

She recognized something in herself that had not been there before, an animal insistence she had at first associated with the girl. A creature's certainty of the enactment of its own nature. So madness, then, where did it lie? With the observer or the observed?

The white wolf said nothing. The white wolf was simply a presence. Simply presence. It would take only the elimination of a word, the dropping of an adverb, the refusal to drop the voice, in order to come to understanding. Understanding appeared from a vantage point. She had to withdraw her vision from down there and allow herself to see from up here. Up here demanded another language altogether. The white wolf was presence. She attempted words. She attempted to speak them aloud. Her mind became whiteness itself, swirling, silent galaxies of light.

Language is a net. It catches you and takes you where it will. Until this moment the woman was still living in the world of words; they trapped her like a specimen. She belonged to them until she saw something, a Presence. Then the poles of her universe shifted instantly so that what had been dry land was flooded with living waters. The Presence was outside of language.

Not graceful like the girl, not simian nor serpentine, but awkward as an old ape, flat teats swinging, without the assistance of true beauty which opens all hearts, the woman made her shaky way along the limb which was biting painfully into her knees and shinbones until she was directly under the apparition of White and prostrated herself best as she could. "Forgive us, Loba," she whispered, "and honor us again with your Presence."

The woman had loved old dogs even when they became bald, when their red skin flaked, when they couldn't romp, when they were incontinent. She had loved them and cared for them. This was the most she would say on her own behalf though she was not asking Loba for any consideration.

Rather she was painfully aware of how unattractive the human body could be when it was not elegantly draped. People instinctively called the police when they saw a naked person. They were offended. It injured their eyes.

She had, herself, once sighted a naked woman walking down the street on a spring afternoon. She neither lowered her eyes nor stared while continuing on her way as if engaged in walking meditation: Breathe in. Breathe out. The mantra she contrived to focus both her mind and her steps didn't serve her but she repeated it nevertheless: Walking on / the dark brown / body of / the Mother. Walking on/ the dark brown .... The woman continued walking toward her.... /Body .... /Body.... She had almost tripped. Of/ ... of... the Mother. Her rhythm was off. No focus could bring it back. The sun gleamed on the woman's ample breasts, on the bowl of her belly, on the sacred triangle of light brown hair with golden strands in it. The Mother was wearing nothing. Nothing. Of the... of the ... of the .... Mother!

"I am so tired of looking for you, of having to track you down," Azul shouted up to the woman as if she was deaf as well as lost. "What are you doing up there? What are you thinking?" Azul was exasperated and stamped her boots.

"I didn't imagine that naked woman. Don't think I'm making her up. The old woman who lived next door had been watering her roses bordering the sidewalk. She grabbed my hand and gasped. I squeezed tight so that she would say nothing until the woman passed us."

"What are you doing, Tecolote?"

"I am thinking about a naked woman I saw once."

"And what are you thinking about her?"

"That she had assumed she was beautiful. I don't think she knew she was naked. She knew she was beautiful and that gave her license. She was wrapped completely in the shimmer of her own mind.

"She passed so close to us without noticing that we were there that I could smell the fresh sweat of her armpits. Not a body that was unwashed or abandoned. A clean body. She had just stepped from a shower you could smell that as well. And now she was taking a vigorous walk and the sweat was beginning to form in her pockets. Sweat and roses. Intoxicating."

"You are beautiful," the girl said, her voice lowering to a pitch between resignation and affection. "Are you going to stay up there long?" The woman herself was so firmly pressed into the tree, out of ardor or fear, that it momentarily amused the girl to imagine that the woman had grown into the tree or it into her, or that the two, woman/tree, using the usual materials, water, fire, earth and air, were configuring a new species all together. A disguise. As if anyone would be distracted by such a deliberate action, or thrown off the trail, by these attempts to disguise the woman's drastic escape from her old life by way of a complete reconfiguration of self. A long thread of a call came from the figure hidden in the branches. The woman was attempting to howl again and the girl heard a response from the surrounding hills. Timber and Frio.

The girl also raised her mouth to the sky and opened it into a fluted goblet as if to catch rain and let her own music fill the air. A mist, indefinable, enveloped them both so much like a perfume that one could not bear taking it in, or being without. A great white shadow appeared to the girl and filled the tree with light. The girl remained still for she could not identify a species by its radiance alone.

The howls resounded from the hills by their house. First Timber, then Frio, then Timber again.

"How long are you going to stay up there? I didn't bring provisions and I don't think you did either. I could go into Carmela's house and bring us something, but I'd rather not. I don't want to have to explain anything to her later."

The girl was not as tender with Owl Woman as she had been with the girl, but that had been a long time ago, another lifetime, the woman thought with satisfaction.

"How long am I going to stay up here? Long enough to know what it was like when we were up here in the beginning before we came down from the trees, before we became so afraid."

"Are you happy up there?"

"Happy? What a strange word. I would never have thought you would use such a word." She considered what the girl was asking her. "Yes. Finally and for the first time, I am happy."

"I'll wait until you're ready to come down, Tecolote," the girl said quietly, folding the woman's clothes she had gathered from under the jade plant, making a seat and pillow out of them. Then she leaned back comfortably against the trunk of the large tree, prepared to wait, if necessary, through the night.

"It's very beautiful up here," the woman said.

*We were born graced by an innate ability to recognize beauty. Some concept of beauty resides in our imagination before we even know the word for beauty. This means that we are born with an innate ability to restore grace to the world in which we live, and to **every living thing** that lives with us, just by the way in which we choose to see.*

— Pami Ozaki

About the Author

Deena Metzger is a writer and healer living at the end of the road in Topanga, California. Her books include the novels *Doors: A Fiction for Jazz Horn*, *The Other Hand*, *What Dinah Thought*, *Skin: Shadows/Silence A Love Letter in the Form of a Novel* and *The Woman Who Slept With Men to Take the War Out of Them* - a novel in the form of a play. The latter is included *Tree: Essays and Pieces*, which features her celebrated Warrior Poster on its cover testifying to a woman's triumph over breast cancer.

Ruin and Beauty: New and Collected Poems is her most recent book. Earlier books of poetry are *A Sabbath Among The Ruins*, *Looking for the Faces of God*, *The Axis Mundi Poems* and *Dark Milk*.

Writing For Your Life: A Guide and Companion to the Inner Worlds is her classic text on writing and the imagination. Two plays *Not As Sleepwalkers* and *Dreams Against the State* have been produced in theaters and various venues. She co-edited the anthology, *Intimate Nature: The Bond Between Women and Animals*, one of the first testimonies to the reality and nature of animal intelligence. *Entering the Ghost River: Meditations on the Theory and Practice of Healing*; and *From Grief into Vision: A Council* examine the tragic failure of contemporary culture and provide guidance for personal, political, environmental and spiritual healing. A radical thinker on behalf of the natural world and planetary survival, a teacher of writing and healing practices for 50 years, a writer and activist profoundly concerned with peacemaking, restoration and sanctuary for a beleagured world, she, with her husband, writer, Michael Ortiz Hill, introduced Daré to North America. Daré is a unique form of individual and community healing based on indigenous and contemporary medicine and wisdom traditions.

A novel, *La Negra y Blanca* is forthcoming from Hand to Hand Publishing in April, 2011. Cherokee is her current four-legged companion.